The Journey Prize Anthology

Winners of the $10,000 Journey Prize

1989
Holley Rubinsky (of Toronto, Ont., and Kaslo, B.C.)
for "Rapid Transits"

1990
Cynthia Flood (of Vancouver, B.C.)
for "My Father Took a Cake to France"

1991
Yann Martel (of Montreal, Que.)
for "The Facts Behind the Helsinki Roccamatios"

1992
Rozena Maart (of Ottawa, Ont.)
for "No Rosa, No District Six"

1993
Gayla Reid (of Vancouver, B.C.)
for "Sister Doyle's Men"

1994
Melissa Hardy (of London, Ont.)
for "Long Man the River"

1995
Kathryn Woodward (of Vancouver, B.C.)
for "Of Marranos and Gilded Angels"

1996
Elyse Gasco (of Montreal, Que.)
for "Can You Wave Bye Bye, Baby?"

The Journey Prize Anthology

Short Fiction from the Best of
Canada's New Writers

Selected with Nino Ricci

M&S

Canadian Cataloguing in Publication Data

The National Library of Canada has catalogued this publication as follows:

Main entry under title:

The Journey Prize anthology:
the best short fiction from Canada's literary journals

Annual.
1–
Subtitle varies.
ISSN 1197-0693
ISBN 0-7710-4425-9 (v. 9)

1. Short stories, Canadian (English).*
2. Canadian fiction (English) – 20th century.*

PS8329.J68   C813'.0108054   C93-039053-9
PR9197.32.J68

Typesetting by M&S

Printed and bound in Canada

The publishers acknowledge the support of the Canada Council for the Arts and the Ontario Arts Council for their publishing program.

McClelland & Stewart Inc.
The Canadian Publishers
481 University Avenue
Toronto, Ontario
M5G 2E9

1 2 3 4 5   01 00 99 98 97

About the Journey Prize Anthology

The $10,000 Journey Prize is awarded annually to a new and developing writer of distinction. This award, now in its ninth year, is made possible by James A. Michener's generous donation of his Canadian royalty earnings from his novel *Journey*, published by McClelland & Stewart Inc. in 1988. The winner of this year's Journey Prize, to be selected from among the twelve stories in this book, will be announced in October 1997 in Toronto as part of the International Festival of Authors.

The Journey Prize Anthology comprises a selection from submissions made by literary journals across Canada, and, in recognition of the vital role journals play in discovering new writers, McClelland & Stewart makes its own award of $2,000 to the journal that has submitted the winning entry.

This year's cover design is by student Clare Robertson, and was selected through a competition held with the Ontario College of Art's third-year design class.

The Journey Prize Anthology has established itself as one of the most prestigious in the country. The anthology has become a who's who of up-and-coming writers, and many of the authors whose early work has appeared in the anthology's pages have gone on to single themselves out with collections of short stories and literary awards. The Journey Prize itself is the most significant monetary award given in Canada to a writer at the beginning of his or her career for a short story or excerpt from a longer fiction work in progress.

McClelland & Stewart would like to acknowledge the continuing enthusiastic support of writers, literary journal editors, and the public in the common celebration of the emergence of new voices in Canadian fiction.

Contents

GABRIELLA GOLIGER

Maladies of the Inner Ear

In the *Hauptmarktplatz* outside Gerda's window all is confusion – whine of engines, slam of metal doors, footsteps, shouts, murmurs, entreaties, cries. She presses her face into the pillow but the din continues. Now the noises order themselves into a steady rhythm, a thick tramp, tramp, tramp of a thousand boots on flagstones; they approach, recede, approach, recede. Sickening as this is, what follows is worse. For now all is still except for the splash of water from the fountain in the middle of the square. It is a tall, spire-shaped masterpiece of intricate stonework, this fountain, the town's showpiece with its tier upon tier of stone figures from the twelfth century. Cascades of water run down the faces and robes of saints, prophets, popes, and noblemen, bathe their stone eyes. Inches from her ear, it seems, water pummels the ground with an incessant smack. She tosses her head sideways. No escape.

In the bedroom of her Cedar Drive luxury apartment, Dr. Gerda Levittson is finally fully awake and staring at a familiar trapezoid of reflected light on the ceiling. The cacophony of the *Hauptmarktplatz* is over, replaced by a shapeless, nameless roaring. Something like a sea is in her head. It thrashes against the walls of her skull with dizzying, deafening force. It is what Gerda calls her demon, and she senses its laughter as she drowns and drowns in noise, is sucked down by foul despair. With an effort she pushes herself into a sitting position. She fumbles in the drawer for her hearing aid and pushes the cool moulded plastic

I

into her ear. As she raps with her knuckles, testing, on the bed-side table, this blessed sound from the outer world penetrates. Tap, tap. A message of hope, calm and real. She switches on the radio. Late night jazz. Muffled trumpet notes above the waves.

Outside, the night is black beyond the glow of the streetlamp. It is two-sixteen a.m. according to her radio clock. The sleeping medication that was supposed to deliver her into morning hasn't worked for some reason. Time, perhaps, to administer a higher dose. Insomnia is the worst part of this affliction that has tormented her for the past two months. Same for everyone. This fact is confirmed not only by the medical journals and textbooks but by the sighs and moans of fellow group members. Those like herself who are new to the misery have the pale, strained faces and nervous tics of insomniacs. Each one hears something different. Mr. Levesque, self-appointed chairman of the group, hears the distant but persistent drone of an airplane. Lucy hears crickets and sometimes, on a very bad day, the sound of smashing china. Another man hears the crackle of radio static, as if his head were caught between channels. "I keep wanting to adjust the dial," he says with a wry grin, while his fingers make a snapping motion in the air.

Gerda switches on the bedside table lamp and attempts to read more of her book, but the words swim on the page and the clamour becomes worse. Learn to live with it, they say in her group. Learn to relax and accept the rushing, roaring wind in the cave as normal and natural as the ticking of a clock, so it abates, becomes background noise and you can hear yourself think. Interesting phrase. Never until now has she realized what it meant, or what its opposite might mean. The steady inner voice that kept her company for seventy-five years, now gone, roughly expelled. She won't find it again until the dawn spreads its calm, grey light through her apartment and solid edges reappear – top of the dresser, silver frame around the family portrait circa 1932 – father, mother, Ludwig, and herself, a plump, bespectacled schoolgirl.

Friday nights back in Germany. The dinner table laden with gilt-edged serving dishes that sent up smells of goulash, sauerkraut,

challah, and wine. Her father with his stern bulldog face sat dis-
tracted, stealing glances at the neatly folded newspaper at his
elbow. Her mother, thin and wan in the light of the Sabbath
candles, was already a sick woman by then. The family was able
to see her safely to her grave before the first volley of boycotts
and decrees.

Ludwig was a grown-up, a teacher at the leading progressive,
secular school. He was remote and handsome with a neat mous-
tache and wavy hair trained back to show off his high, noble forehead. With his confident laugh, he teased her about what she
didn't remember or hadn't yet learned. He recited Heine: "Oh
Germany, distant love of mine. . . . Well, what comes next?" Her
cheeks flushed with indignation. She could have told him about
the life cycle of the honeybee, but he asked the wrong questions.

Her father mumbled his high-speed version of *Birkat
Hamazon*, Grace After Meals. "Lord our God . . . sustains the
whole world . . . food to all creatures . . . may the Merciful One
reign. . . ."

Before the amen, and despite entreaties from their mother,
Ludwig was up from his chair and dashing towards the hall.

"What a way to behave. You'll spoil your digestion."

He sat his fedora on his head, blew a kiss, and was gone. They
knew where he was off to, the *Hauptmarktplatz*, where the
young folks gathered on Friday and Saturday nights to exchange
news and argue politics but mostly to flirt and to court or be
courted. Arm in arm, newly matched couples paraded around
the perimeter of the square while those still single clustered in
small groups by the fountain. Ludwig was in high demand.

It is dark. It is the middle of the night. Outside, beyond Cedar
Drive, the woods of Mount Royal lie still in the heavy August
air. The sweet, rotting smell of late August wafts through the
window. She would like to walk outside right now into the
embrace of the bathwater warm air in her nightgown but . . .
muggers and maniacs. This too is new, this timidity. A few
months ago, Dr. Gerda Levittson, despite her age, her deafness,
her cane, walked the most secluded paths of Mount Royal
whenever she pleased. Former patients, whose faces she always

remembered although she forgot their names, greeted her with delight. "It's just not the same since you retired," an old-timer would say. "The young ones these days don't know how to listen."

Her hair was still red then. She went once a month to Celine at Salon Ultra to have her favourite colour, Sunset Glow, reapplied by Celine's deft hands. Afterwards, as she stumped along through the crowds of St. Catherine Street, she chuckled to herself at the occasional startled glance or indulgent smile she received. That wonderful parade of fashionable young people in their leathers and silks and studied indifference.

She has lost heart for the Ultra and St. Catherine Street. The hairdryer bothers her now, the smells, and most of all being confined in the chair with the hot, sticky plastic apron tied tight around her neck. She wonders whether, beneath the cooing encouragement, Celine has been laughing at her all these years. Her real colour, yellowish-grey, has grown back in, pushing the band of orange-red away from her head and looking, for the first few weeks, like a gaudy, badly arranged bandanna.

She reaches under the bed for her notepad and pen to work on the little talk on medications she is preparing for her group. "Help from Medicine," she has written. "Tinnitus. From the Latin. Meaning to toll or ring like a bell. Can be almost any kind of noise – a hissing, whistling, crackling, grinding, roaring, thrumming, clicking, chirping, pulsing, rattling, booming, or any combination of these, or even a tune, endlessly, distractingly repeated. A symptom, not a disease. Some possible causes: An increase of fluid in the inner ear, pressure on nerve fibres due to infections, tumours, multiple sclerosis, muscular spasms, circulation problems, reactions to drugs, caffeine, alcohol, loud noises, hormonal changes, anxiety, depression, shock."

Two-thirty a.m. The endless night creeps on its belly.

Back in Nürnberg her family kept the commandments. In moderation and in the time-honoured, respectable, decorum-loving way of the German-Jewish bourgeoisie. They lit candles, ate the Sabbath meal, and closed the store on Saturday. But instead of synagogue service, Anton, her father, went in to do accounts in the shuttered gloom of the store or to sort through boxes. Sometimes he took Gerda along, hoping to give her at least a taste for the business since Ludwig had turned out hopeless, but also to keep her out of her mother's hair. Else Levittson needed her Sabbath morning rest.

Gerda would sit on the floor in the crowded aisle, fingering the goods – patent leather, suede, and crocodile skin handbags, kid gloves, wallets, umbrellas. Rich leather smells. Her father would emerge from the storeroom, sweating and in shirtsleeves, to show her the latest luxury item from South America.

"Look at this. Iguana. Beautiful, no?"

She examined the soft, miniature scales of the iguana-skin purse, how they overlapped. She squinted down at her own skin that was more like the tanned leather of the belts and handbags, crisscrossed with a million fine lines forming tiny triangles. Why? She puzzled.

At what point did she forget to think about Ludwig? Was it when she and her father walked in a daze down the gangplank into the Montreal harbour? It was sheer luck they got out when they did. One moment they were like all the other lost souls without papers, scurrying along the streets, ducking their heads when a Brownshirt appeared. Then, a miracle. A visitor's permit to England and later the boat tickets from cousin Sheldon in Montreal. The last they saw Ludwig he was in his cellar flat in Berlin, chain smoking at the kitchen table, his blue eyes confused and sad. A brief, proud light flared back up in them when his father tried to persuade him to leave. He could not face more grovelling in the anterooms of consulates. He was determined to wait the Nazis out.

Ludwig slipped from her mind somehow, and at that moment, it would seem, a cattlecar door clanged shut. Insane thought, outrageous and utterly symptomatic, according to the psychologists. She cannot bring herself to think beyond the slamming of the door. The door shuts and her mind retreats and she is relieved at her lack of morbidity and she is aghast at her cowardice and it goes around and around. A textbook case. Still, she searches for the moment of forgetfulness. She pieces together the old apartment on Queen Mary Road, her father's bedroom, her study where the radiators in winter gave off too much heat and she sat near an open window letting gusts of wind keep her awake.

She loved the lonely night hours. Fifty years ago Gerda Levittson, the McGill medical student living in her father's house, itched for eleven o'clock, for the dreary Friday evening Sabbath ritual to be over and for her father to plod down the corridor to his bed. Then, laying a towel along the bottom of the door to prevent light from spilling into the hall and arousing her father's peevish anger, she switched on the desk lamp. That fine, intense glare on the textbook print. She tunnelled down, noted, memorized, added knowledge, brick by brick, to her solid foundations. The late night stillness was immense and calm, buoyed her up. She lifted her head from her books and felt it press against her. Solitude was a muscular embrace.

The dining room in the Queen Mary Road apartment. Cluttered with unnecessary sideboards and chairs where she and her father sat crowded amid the serving dishes on Friday nights. When did her father go back to the strict orthodoxy of his childhood? After the Red Cross telegram, or before? One day when she'd come back from a lab, a gleaming set of crockery, uncontaminated and ready for the new kosher regime, stood on the kitchen counter. A long list of injunctions went with it. On the Sabbath she was not to turn on a light, not to tear a page, not to put pen to paper, not to ride, not to carry any object – not even a book – outside the house. A prayer for rising and for lying down to sleep. A benediction for hearing good tidings and for hearing bad. A chain-link fence of rituals and commandments that invested the minutiae of daily life with enormous significance and kept everything outside at bay. The quaver in her father's voice as he laid down the law, made Gerda go along with it while she planned her escapes and respites. How Ludwig might have teased and waggled a forefinger. "Have you said your benediction for slicing into a cadaver?"

Her father cooked and cleaned while Gerda went to her classes at McGill. On Fridays she had to be home in time for the lighting of the candles. When she arrived he was wearing a velvet skullcap – special for Shabbas – on his bald, liver-spotted head, and it made his jowly face look more withered and pathetic than ever.

He fussed, he shuffled between dining room and kitchen preparing the table – challah and challah cover, kiddush cup, salt cellar, prayer book, dishes and cutlery. His aged hand held the kiddush cup in the air, the dark wine trembling at the brim as he recited the blessing in a gravelly voice. He did the *Motzi*, blessing over bread. Slowly his stiff fingers tore off a piece from the challah loaf for her, sprinkled salt, and placed it by her plate.

When she opened her mouth to say something his hand flew to his face in an alarmed gesture. No talking between kiddush and *Motzi*, she remembered. As she ate her salted bread, he hurried to the kitchen to bring out the meal. A pale chicken broth with bits of parsley and droplets of fat as his own mother used to make. Roast chicken, potato dumplings, peas and beets. The same dinner repeated itself every Friday, down to the canned dessert peaches and vanilla wafers, imported from Israel. He munched in silence, methodically, without any sign of pleasure or appetite. After sopping the last bit of gravy from his plate with his bread, he launched into a rambling monologue about arcane family customs.

"In your Aunt Rebecca's house they took their salt from a little crystal dish. Do you remember? No, you were too young. A silver and crystal dish, part of a set she had from the Frankfurt side of the family. They took a pinch between forefinger and thumb and sprinkled it on the challah. Like this, see? My mother thought it uncivilized, everyone dipping their fingers in the same dish. But Rebecca said hers was the more traditional way. The thing is, now I don't know which is right. . . ." His voice trailed off, thin and plaintive.

"Ask a rabbi," Gerda said, her eye on the clock.

"Ach, the rabbis here. Polacks and Russians. They know things, of course. But it's not the same as a rabbi from home."

Finally, he droned out Grace after Meals. ". . . for your covenant which you sealed in our flesh; for your Torah . . . for your laws . . .

for life, grace and kindness. . . ." His voice was a flat monotone. He couldn't carry the tune at the singing parts, but did not seem to expect her to help out. At the last words he rapped on the table. "*Pflicht getan.*" Duty done.

"Insomnia," she writes in her notebook. "The most trouble-some effect. Medications: anti-spasmodic clonazepan (brand name Rivotril) . . . the tricyclic amitriptyline . . . A specialist from New Zealand prescribes an anti-convulsive. . . ."

The group members are proud to have her in their midst. They look to her for answers. "I know nothing more than you do. There is little substantial research. . . ." No matter. They describe symptoms and wait for her answers. Often she walks out of the meeting more dazed and battered than when she came in. Still she regards the meetings every second Thursday as a necessity. These fellow shipwrecked travellers. They know, they hear. In their strained smiles and anxious eyes she sees the reflection of her own pain. It is as necessary to be in contact with them as to locate familiar objects in her room after troubled sleep. She envies them their simple-minded credulity. They are eager to try herbal remedies, sound masking devices, reflex-ology, colour therapy, acupuncture, although, from what Gerda can tell, the results of these treatments are highly inconclusive.

"Chronic tinnitus is chronic pain. Our nervous systems are not adapted to absorb the impact of a constant stimulus. Internally generated sound, from which there is no escape, cre-ates an abnormal situation that can call forth the production of noradrenaline, a neuro-chemical that primes our responses. . . ." The nerve endings in the inner ear quiver. They cannot stop. Their bath of liquid is in perpetual motion.

One of the more bizarre theories to float out of the pages of the *Volkischer Beobachter* soon after the Nazis took power was that you could distinguish Jew from Aryan by the shape of the left ear. Ludwig snorted with delight when he heard about this. He had a photo taken of himself in left profile and sent it, under the pseudonym Reiner Deutschmann, to the editor. An example of the impeccable Aryan ear. They printed it, with thanks. Ludwig was on top of the world.

The telegram from the British Red Cross was as brief and final as words on a tomb. "Ludwig Levittson last seen Berlin February 1943 boarding transport. Destination eastern territories. Regret no further information at this time." A scrap of newsprint paper with three badly typed lines, large Xs over the mistakes, and the date on top – September 5, 1946. The end of almost ten years of anxious inquiries, nightmarish rumours, a clutching at hopeful signs, and a growing certainty of doom. She put it in the file folder marked "Red Cross," which she slipped in at the back of the cabinet drawer.

Her father sat hunched at the end of his bed, his hands limp in his lap, tears dripping from his nose and chin. First he'd waved the brutal truth away. The telegram was vague, so sparse in detail, after all. What kind of transport and which part of the East, could the Red Cross not find out, could it not have been possible . . .? Gerda shook her head, grim, determined to end this futile hanging on, this water torture of letters to officials and their carefully worded replies. Finally, he crumpled up and wept, resigned, helpless, exhausted, unrestrained. While horrified at their abundance, Gerda envied him his simple flood of tears. It seemed he would cry the life out of himself. She stroked his shoulders and head, rocked him in her arms, averting her face from his wet, loose cheeks, their odour of age and despair.

As he wept, she planned the days ahead. Her first term of medical school was about to begin. She could not afford to miss a lecture but could put off long study sessions for a couple of weeks while she kept him company until the worst was over. Then she must cut along her own life's course.

During the months that followed, she prepared for mid-term exams. She ignored the silence that fell and the burst of chatter that rose up again like a wall when she walked into the med school cafeteria. All those male voices linked in cama-raderie and common disdain. She bent her burning cheeks towards her books.

At night, when her overheated brain would not shut down, she would pick up the anatomy text at her bedside table. She'd trace the course of blood through the body, enumerate out loud the soothing names of the chambers of the heart. Superior vena cava, inferior vena cava. Atrium, atrio-ventricular valve. Aorta to arteries to minute capillaries where the blood cells push through, one by one by one, transform themselves through intricate chemical reactions, then carry on their timeless and perfect journey back to the heart.

Words roll and buckle on the page. Metal gates crash, smash against tender membranes already whipped raw. Noise is pain is noise and she is buried in it, six feet under, mouth, nose, ears stuffed with smash, crash, and the yowl of the dead. This is not madness, it's a condition, it's all the same.

"Enough now. Stop." Her frail, cracked voice takes aim at the bedlam. "Enough of this nonsense."

She reads aloud. She recites: "*Yitgadal veyitkadash shemei raba. . . .* If I forget you, O Jerusalem. . . ." Whatever words come to hand until she stands solid again above the waves. "Tinnitus, from the Latin, meaning to ring or toll like a bell. . . ."

The young ones these days don't know how to listen. Was she a good listener? Was she, really? She certainly knew how to translate the anguished but vague complaints into precise symptoms. The file on Mr. X.Y.Z. grew fat. Symptoms noted, tests ordered, results collected, medications prescribed, side-effects noted, medications changed.

Another scorcher, the radio announcer promises. The sky, glimpsed through the curtains of the kitchen window, has gone from black to milky grey. Streetlights wink off, bringing the daytime world into faint but unmistakable relief. Later on, the street will lie in dusty, yellow heat, but for now a pleasant breeze parts the kitchen curtains and caresses her face. The ocean roar is beginning to subside. Gerda sips scalding hot camomile tea to soothe her stomach, which threatens to heave bile. Every bodily function now – a stubborn bowel movement, a fit of tears – can start up the tidal wave in her head again. She takes small, wary sips. The stomach above all is a capricious beast that must be treated with respect.

Across the hall, the soft click of a neighbour's door. Gerda opens her own door to greet Mrs. Paulsen, a pink-cheeked woman about Gerda's age, but younger looking, who is on her way to the garbage chute. Mrs. Paulsen's eyes, limpid and innocent, show that she takes the calm around her for granted. Her movements cause no reverberations. She could not even guess at the shroud of echoes that Gerda carries, although she has clicked her tongue and shaken her head over Gerda's descriptions.

Back in the apartment Gerda listens to the radio announcers, a man and a woman, who chatter about flooding in the Milon Tunnel and a stalled truck that's spilled its load of hamburger buns onto the Décarie Expressway. Morning sounds. A miracle of solid ground through the waves.

Who is she to deserve miracles?

She closes her eyes for just one instant, her attention wanders, and look what happens. A row of naked, emaciated men totters above a ditch, topples down into the cold ooze, their mouths open but soundless, their eyes crying out an unspeakable horror. If she had kept that fine-tooled mind more alert, if she had hearkened for the clanging of the gate. . . .

She continues writing: "Some people find relief through various treatments . . . masking devices that generate 'white noise' . . . cassette tapes with environmental sounds such as ocean waves breaking on a shore."

There is no cure. Slowly the mind flattens itself, adjusts, yields to the pounding wash. Slowly, sound and silence are one. A firmament appears on the surface of the waters.

DENNIS BOCK

Olympia

Only what is entirely lost demands to be endlessly named.
— Günter Grass

What was water for us that summer but a prison? Almost a year to the day after my grandmother drowned in a boating accident, my uncle Günter came to visit us from Germany and found cracks at the bottom of our swimming pool. This was August 1972, the summer water would almost kill me. First because there wasn't enough of it; and later because it almost took me the same as it had taken my grandmother.

I'd heard stories about Günter, my mother's brother. What he was like when they were kids. War stories, water stories. They'd all lived through the war. My father, too. I was raised by war babies. Everybody with their story, their dry silence. Friends of my parents, the teller from Frankfurt who worked at the Bank of Montreal on Lakeshore and Charles and spoke to my father in whispers over folded fives and twenties. They all came out of that experience, had left it as soon as they could to come to this country. But now I know no one was ever able to leave it behind fully, though it took me until that summer to find that out. Once, long before that summer, my mother explained to me that she'd come here from a dark country. I thought she'd meant the weather, lack of sunshine, too much rain.

She spent her war years in the north of Germany, trapped there, among falling bombs. She told me about brushing her teeth with salt, the constant drought under her tongue, how they ate nothing but salted cabbage, about the dead man who fell from the sky and lay in the front yard of their house through the month of May and into June, how an old woman from the neighbourhood came by with a bucket of salt every week and sprinkled it over the body to keep the fumes down until the town came and took him away.

She, my uncle, and their mother – the father already half dead in the salt mines near Odessa, the mineral of dehydration sucking the liquids through his skin, his eyeballs, bringing his lungs, his hunger to the ridge of his teeth. The three of them, six months in a basement. And when the end finally came, collected onto rail cars and rolled over the great smouldering landscape to the shores of the Gulf of Riga where they were released like sickly cattle into a February blizzard. Then hopping freight cars to get back, holding her little brother's hand dry with fear as they ran, and she the hand of her mother, the three of them grasping for the invisible hand that reached from the tousled boards of departing freight cars and missing, always missing that train, that hand, walking and waiting and running again. Four months to return home and nothing left but stories. Stories to burn. Drought stories. Stories of salt. Stories that in my boyhood meant as much to me as television, as the map of the untravelled world.

Before Uncle Günter came that summer, I found purpose in the meaning of those stories. Even then I used them to protect me. I needed the train story because of the words *cattle car. Freight car*. The salt stories didn't occur to me until I saw Günter down there at the bottom of our bone-dry swimming pool. I didn't understand the salt then, what the drought behind my mother's tongue meant, behind her brother's eyes. It was the trains I saw them ride up to the hanging lip of Sweden. We were learning about the Holocaust in school, seeing films of Jews as they rolled into Auschwitz, thousands of them at a time, on cattle cars. Freight cars. The image of my mother and her little brother aboard one of those cars shining in my head as brightly as they shot out from those dark spinning reels at the back of the classroom melded with stories of displacement and organized death. After history class I dreamt my mother came to me with forgiveness, sometimes offering it. "Sweetheart," she said. "We all suffered. No one person more than the next." But in my dreams and in my waking life I didn't believe her. I'd seen those films of men and women, ghosts already, waiting to die. I used my mother's story, told it to my teachers and to anyone who would listen, used it to show how my people had paid. But I knew they hadn't paid enough.

She was losing water. The summer drought had already been declared. It was in early August, when my uncle and Monika came to Oak Park to spend the summer with us, that we realized where the problem lay. Hairline cracks, practically invisible, were spreading like transparent veins along the walls and the bottom.

Uncle Günter and his wife Monika were from Fürstenfeld-bruck, a small town outside of Munich. In the letters we got before they arrived they said they planned to stay with us for six weeks, with a weekend trip here and there around the province and down into New York. They wanted to get away from Munich before the Olympic Games quadrupled the size of their town. But once Uncle Günter saw the condition our pool was in, he wanted to crawl down to the bottom and begin repairing those invisible cracks, a job, he assured my parents, that would take three, maybe four days. That's how he came to dominate our summer the way he did, to prolong our thirst.

Günter and Monika spoke German with my parents, although when Ruby and I were around – which was most of the time – Monika spoke English to us in a British accent. She sounded like Diana Rigg from *The Avengers*. She had spent the war years in England. Günter's English wasn't as good as my parents'. I'd long since been unable to hear their accent, but during open house at school and around the neighbourhood I knew it revealed them as the immigrants they were, the tellers of war stories.

Everything I saw in Günter, everything he did that summer, everything I heard him say – in German and in his broken English – I attributed to the war. The war had shaped him like it had not shaped, could never shape, my mother. He was tall, taller than my father, and had a sunken chest that looked as though it were pushing the life out of his heart and lungs. At school we called kids like him *fish eyes*. He didn't look at you so much as stare, blinking uncontrollably over those protruding, round mirrors. He was a construction worker, his large calloused hands constantly moving at his sides like the sands of a shifting desert floor.

When we got home after picking them up at the airport, we walked them around the house, showed them the guest room with the view to the street and a thin slice of Lake Ontario, her winding shoreline already receding for the dry air that had been haunting our summer. We took them into the back yard, where my mother showed them her garden. Ruby and I followed behind at a safe distance, listening to their foreign voices and punching each other in the arm. My mother pulled aside the browning rhubarb leaves she'd been trying to keep alive beside the peach tree and offered up a sniff of hard Ontario soil to her brother's nose. I watched him sniff a stream of dust. His fish eyes rolled back into his head. It looked like he was going to hurt himself, but he inhaled again, even deeper. Breathing in the dust. *This* was my mother's brother? I thought. My uncle? I watched his eyes roll back around to the world, to me, and a smile pull at his mouth and cheeks. Ruby gave me a shot in the shoulder and took off round the house.

The five of us walked across the grass and looked down into the dry pit of our swimming pool. My father was the Mister Fix-It of the family. That spring he'd repaired all the eaves on our house in one day. But he said he didn't have time to replaster the whole pool.

"*Ich habe keine Zeit fur solche Blöde Sachen,*" he said, pointing over the dry hole and looking at his in-laws.

After he said that, Uncle Günter jumped down onto the blue cement of the shallow end, got down on his knees, and started running his hands over the walls and floor. Then he slid on his haunches down into the deep end and did the same thing. When he climbed back up onto the deck and started talking in German, I heard my mother and father begin to say *no* again and again, no way, that much I could tell, *nein, nein, nein*, but Günter shook his head and smiled and rubbed his dry hands together. Monika stood beside me, frowning, but why . . . I couldn't tell.

Günter was bent on fixing our pool. He'd flown here with his wife to visit his only sister and the brother-in-law he'd never met before, their two children, and he wanted to start out his vacation at the bottom of a dried-out hole in the ground. My mother and father didn't like the idea. They were mystified. Uncomfortable. That's not why he'd come, they reminded him. But when they found him down there the next morning slowly sanding the chlorine film and dried algae off the walls, they couldn't coax him out.

"Okay," my mother said later that morning on the deck, look-ing down, a cup of coffee in her hand. In English. "A day or two of this, then the vacation starts." Günter looked up and smiled.

"Maybe this is his way of getting over culture-shock," my father said on the front porch the second night after Uncle Günter and Monika had gone to bed. I was upstairs in my mother's sewing room, my head pushed out into the night. "It'll pass. He'll snap out of it soon."

The great unknown in Munich was who would take home the most medals, how many consecutive back flips Olga Korbut could manage before she spun off into the clouds. The sound of my uncle working in the back yard drifted through the open living room window while Ruby and I, dressed in matching track suits, watched the Games. We were both going to be Olympic gymnasts. Ruby, her chest pressed low to the floor, her chin cupped in her hands, studied the impossible postures of her heroes. She sat in the splits for hours at a time. I did fifty push-ups every morning and held handstands during commercials. The Canadian team was twelfth out of fifteen. I fantasized about how things would be different if I'd been born Romanian or Russian or Japanese, how I'd be competing, and winning. Anything but who I was.

Around our house that summer the great mystery was how long Günter could sit at the bottom of our pool, drinking cups of coffee prepared for him by my mother and saying to himself, *"Verflixt heiss!"* as he dragged his plaster-covered sleeve across his forehead. Every afternoon when my father got home from work he found Günter in the kitchen leaning against the counter drinking coffee, the peach or gooseberry or rhubarb pie my mother had made for that evening's dessert sitting half-eaten on the table. In the next room Ruby and I dreamed of gold medals and of our first real swim of the summer. It was hot, hadn't rained since early July. And at five-thirty I watched a frown fall over my father's face as he walked past us all on his way to the bathroom to get cleaned up before supper.

I felt the tension seep through the wall of that foreign language that first Saturday with my uncle and Monika. It was a hot and sticky evening. We ate at the picnic table under the tall pines in the back yard. I felt something when my mother and Günter spoke to each other, me on the other side, as clearly as a hand brushing over my face. But as subtly, as indistinctly as the water had drained from the shell of our pool. I imagined it was because he'd insisted on fixing the pool, was denying something of her hospitality.

"Beautiful," my father said. I bit into my hamburger. "One of the biggest jobs we've ever done." He began telling us about the boat he was working on at the shop, a sixty-footer on order from Bermuda. Then, for Günter's sake, he started in German. I chewed as he spoke, counting in my head the number of medals the Bermudan team had won so far. Monika sat across from me. I put down my burger, reached for the wine bottle beside her plate, filled her glass. My mother was always reminding us to be polite. She pulled her long hair behind her ear, touched my arm to say enough. Her touch ran to the pit of my stomach like a vein of butterflies. My uncle looked at me from the other end of the table. I blushed. My father stopped.

"We got a bronze in sailing today," I said, clearing my throat. "Soling class." Monika looked at me blankly. "Three-man keel-boat," as if to reassure her. "You guys got a bronze in the Flying Dutchman class." I looked at Günter when I said, *You guys*.

Blushed again. Monika had a beautiful face. There was a silence. She looked at me and pulled her hair back behind her right ear again. Women my mother's age never wore their hair below the shoulder. My uncle sipped his wine. My mother looked at me, smiled a little.

"Looks like we're neck on neck," my father said. Coming back out to English.

I think my father was the first one to see how things were going to go between my mother and uncle. The next evening, when the silence came, he quickly asked Ruby and me to put on our own little Olympiad. Right there, in the middle of dinner. "Okay," Ruby said happily, without any coaxing, and bounced across the parched grass before our mother could protest, cart-wheeling and back-flipping and spinning through the air. When she came to a stop, panting and smiling, she threw her arms up to the sky and thrust out her small chest. My father stood up in his seat. "The judge in blue concedes a perfect ten." When she came back to the table, I jumped up onto my hands, the world turned upside down, the grass suddenly my sky, and held the earth against my palms and fingers for as long as I could. Atlas inverted, and saw my uncle staring at me stone-faced.

Ruby scored higher than I did, but I knew that was because she was younger, that our mini-Olympics were meant to bring us together, to head off something coming between my mother and my uncle. And for a while they did. Monika ended up sitting in a lawn chair out on the grass with her wine glass hanging low to the ground, whistling out scores along with my parents. The August light began to fold in upon itself and the distinct knock of a croquet ball flew up from behind the cedar fence of the neighbour's yard like a startled sparrow. But when I let go of the earth for the last time that night and returned to my feet, blood resuming its equilibrium, my uncle was gone.

We began clearing away the table, everyone except Uncle Günter taking his or her share back to the kitchen. He was standing out on the front porch, alone, his hands in his pockets. I saw him there when I delivered my first load of dishes. Back out by the picnic table, I saw my father walk over the lawn and pause at the edge of the dry swimming pool, looking down at the hard, cracking cement. I watched his face drain of all joy that had filled him at our performance, all pleasure that had been his, as if that empty hole in the ground were sucking up his livelihood and his pride. No one else seemed to notice my father's grief the first night he stood at the edge of the pool shaking his head in disbelief; no one noticed that night how that empty pool drained the life out of him. At the time I didn't think my father's melancholy had anything to do with Uncle Günter's slow work, or the tension between my mother and my uncle. I thought it was my grandmother. How she'd drowned the day of her fortieth wedding anniversary, the day she and my grandfather had chosen to renew their vows. I guessed he was looking for her down there in some way, that these people had brought from Germany unwanted memories, unwanted stories along with their appetite for wine and reparations. I guessed he was thinking about losing his mom.

By late August Olga Korbut was wowing the whole world, and Uncle Günter was up to eight coffee breaks a day. He wanted to stay down there. Working and standing around. My mother and father wanted him out. Monika had taken to borrowing the Chrysler and disappearing every day. I guessed she'd had enough of waiting for Günter. She drove to the Elora Gorge, Niagara Falls, Detroit, and Ithaca. She went to Toronto a couple of times a week, to London, to Kingston and the Thousand Islands. When she was gone, when an event Ruby and I didn't much care for came on TV, we went out to the back yard, hung our feet over the side, and watched our uncle stand around at the bottom of the pool. On the grass we played under the sprinkler to bring home to him our desperation, our need of water. I thought the pool would remain dry forever. All day I walked around the house drinking glasses of water. Günter had become a fixture down there, his trowel, the cement mixer my father had reluctantly borrowed from a friend from work, the three moon-eyed bubbles of the level watching his slow dance among the forgotten artifacts at the bottom of a dried sea.

One day, after playing in the sprinkler, we sat on the deck with our glasses of water and listened to Günter speak to us.

Neither of us understood a word. For the whole afternoon he told us what sounded like stories. We sat there, embarrassed to stop him, forced to listen to the end of his ramblings, sipping, forever sipping. Sometimes as he spoke he became angry and then immediately fell silent, or laughed and slapped an open palm on his thigh. We sat at the edge of the hole in the ground and watched him move slowly like a lion in a pit among his tools, picking things up and examining them, holding them against the sun over our heads as he spoke, then gently returning them to where they had been. Transfixed, parched, clouds of dry cement dust mushrooming and rising from the bottom of the pool, caking our throats as we watched him cover palm-sized patches of the pool as if he were painting a white curtain over an old movie set from 20,000 *Leagues Under the Sea.*

On a Saturday night in late August, after Günter and Monika had been with us for three weeks, my parents left me in charge of Ruby. They took Uncle Günter into the city to go dancing at Club Edelweiss, a German-Canadian restaurant where my father sometimes played accordion with a band, or soloed for small parties. Günter reluctantly agreed to go. Monika didn't. She said she was tired from her day of sightseeing. She sat on the front porch with Ruby, a glass of wine in her hand, and waved good-bye when the car pulled out of the driveway. I went around the back and climbed into the dry pool for the first time.

I jumped down into the shallow end, like Günter had that first day, and began to explore. I wanted to go deep, to find out something about my mother's brother. I knew nothing but the war stories, the outstretched hands reaching for freight trains. In our school history text, I'd read about the Potsdam Conference, the great shifting of borders after the Control Council agreed to deport more than six million Germans beyond the Oder-Neisse line. The uprooting of my mother's people. I slid down the dusty incline on my haunches and felt the sides of the pool squeeze the world into a box of evening sky above my head. At my feet extension cords twisted like snakes, trowels flat and stupid-looking, a sawhorse, the three-foot level, a half-used bag of cement, and an old red toolbox. Mostly my father's things, other things, tools borrowed from his friends.

"You don't want to be anything like him, do you?"

I looked up. The sun was setting behind the apartments across the street from the house. A last shaft of light spiralled between the buildings and lit up Monika's face at a ninety-degree angle, and collected in the glass of wine in her right hand. "What's down there for you?" she said.

"I dropped something."

"Well, get it quick and get back up here or he'll rub off on you." Then she walked away.

In the kitchen the next day, while I was getting a handful of cookies for Ruby and me, Günter walked in and said in his broken English, "I need help. Come here." I didn't answer him. He poured himself a glass of lemonade, drank it down, and walked out of the kitchen. I followed him into the back yard, jumped down into the shallow end, and felt the cookies in my pocket snap into little bits.

"You a smart boy?"

I nodded. "Not very good with my hands."

"Hold this," and handed me a trowel. "Make so." He started smoothing cement along the north wall of the deep end. I watched him for a minute. He started whistling. Then he stopped and turned to me. "*Ja?*"

I stooped over, took some plaster onto my trowel, and stepped up to the nearest wall. I hesitated. I thought of what Monika had said. Him rubbing off on me. Just a strange man, I thought. He was my mother's brother, after all. How would you want him to treat you in his country? I remembered my mother asking me in the car as we drove to the airport to pick them up.

"You watch too much TV," he said.

I began spreading the cement.

"The Olympics are important. Family of Nations."

Then, his face to the spreading curtain, he said, "Okay, get lost."

Into the fourth week of the visit – during which not an ounce of rain had fallen from the sky – my mother told us on a Saturday morning that we were going to Kelso. We were going to find water. We were going to bathe in clean cool water.

The artificial lake is the main attraction at Kelso. There are two beaches on the south shore, divided by a grassy hill on top of which sits a parking lot and, on the opposite slope, the outfitters where my father and I had, on a couple of occasions, rented a sailboat. No matter how hard the sun comes down on you there, no matter which shore you stand on, you can always hear the traffic going by on the highway just beyond the poplar and spruce trees on the north hill. There are rainbow in the lake, too, but I'd never caught anything other than rock bass and sun fish, though I'd always wanted to catch a trout. That Saturday I brought my fishing rod along with me just in case.

After we got organized in the parking lot, unloaded the picnic baskets and towels and parasol and magazines and my fishing rod, the six of us walked down the wooden stairs to the beach like three distinct couples. Monika, her large floppy sun hat flapping like a bird, walked a step ahead of her husband. He looked sullen, hadn't spoken in the car the whole way up. My mother seemed nervous. She swung the picnic basket about grandly from hand to hand, distracting attention from something. Was she thinking about her brother? Then I wondered if it was the memory of last summer that was bothering her, if she was worried about my father. If this trip to water would trigger the memory of his mother's drowning. But my father joked with Ruby and me as we walked down the wooden stairs. On the way here he'd worn a pair of black sunglasses. Ruby said he looked like a gangster. Halfway down the stairs he turned around to us, his rolled-up towel hidden clumsily under his baggy summer shirt like a bag of money, and said in a terrible Italian accent, "Meester Capone wantsa you to doa littlea favore fora la Familia," and Ruby laughed and jumped up for his glasses like a little barking dog. I carried the rod and tackle and the second lunch basket. We'd all changed into our bathing suits at home.

We found an empty stretch of sand at the far end of the first beach, close to an old man and woman. Someone's grandparents,

I could tell. But they were alone. No kids. No grandkids. Their loose skin covered their bodies like a fluorescent wrap. My father and I smoothed out the hot sand with our bare feet. We laid out our clean, bleached towels side by side, six in a row like the colourful stained-glass windows of a church. We peeled off our street clothes, settled down, and waited to get hot enough to go in. Ruby went down to the shore and waded in up to her knees to check the water.

My towel was beside Monika. "Have you caught fish in here?"

"Some," I said. Her legs stretched out beside me. She was wearing a bikini. Her long brown hair shone in the sun. My mother always wore a one-piece. No mothers on the beach wore bikinis. No other women had long hair. Monika had never had a baby. Her stomach was flat and her legs were still slender. She was twirling a long brown lock in her fingers, her eyes closed, right knee raised slightly in the air, her breasts puffing apart from the centre of her chest in a way that made me want to keep looking. She asked me the question about the fish without opening her eyes, without looking at me. Then I saw my uncle watching me over the rim of his sunglasses. I turned away and faced the lake.

There were a lot of people swimming, splashing around on inflatable mattresses and dinghies. I walked alone along the edge of the water. Monika, I thought. Had Günter known what I was thinking? I watched the red and blue sailboats, their white hulls pulled up on the wind, shining against the water. I watched them pick up speed and skim across the small lake, lowered because of the drought, and then, trapped, tack back against the wind. I tried thinking about sailing, about the fishing I would do later that afternoon, about gymnastics. But Monika kept coming back to me. I entered the shade of the woods and leaned my back against an elm and looked for Monika's pink skin among the crowd in the distance. I waited under an overhanging elm branch, hoping, impossibly, that she'd come to me into the dark woods, that she'd join me, leave my uncle, that old blinking lion from the bottom of our swimming pool. I waited. I put my hand down the front of my bathing suit. The sight of Monika in the lawn chair as I'd stood on my head, her long legs crossed like I thought only movie stars crossed their legs, calling out scores, the glass of wine hanging low to the ground before she raised it to her red lips. The sight of her on the beach, her bikini, long hair, the way her breasts hung away from her, one towards me, the other off on its own, its hard dark eye staring down a lucky admirer.

I walked into the sunlight again, over the sand and back to the blankets. Everybody was in the water except my uncle. My father yelled to me when he saw me, called for me to come in. Uncle Günter sat watching, all alone with his sunglasses pulled up over his face. I waded in and cleaned my hands in the water.

After lunch I took my fishing rod and tackle to the other end of the lake and fished the small stream that fed the reservoir. From there I could see the two beaches stretched out over the opposite shoreline like strips of bark pulled from a tree, the hill rising between them like a broad nose. With my hands I dug up some worms, put them in the small plastic container I kept in my tackle box and slid the first worm along a size fourteen hook. I threw it out into a pool and let the worm sink to the bottom. I caught a trout for the first time in my life. Slick and spotted. He was beautiful. I killed him with my pen knife and dropped him into a plastic bag. He wasn't a prize, but he was big enough to keep. In an hour I caught three more pan-size rainbows. Before leaving the stream I rinsed the blood off the fish and rinsed out the bag. I carried the plastic bag in my left hand as I walked back to the beach. It thumped against my thigh with every step. By the time I got back a little puddle of blood had formed in the heavier corner of the bag.

When I held it up for everyone to see, Ruby made silly noises and plugged her nose. My mother peered her eyes down over the lip of stretched plastic. I told my father what I'd used, what part of the stream I'd fished, how each fish had hit, which was the best fighter. Monika leaned on an elbow, listening. I described how I'd moved each one to the top of the pool and enticed them to jump by lifting the tip of the rod against the sky. The old couple listened to my story from the next set of beach towels. My mother emptied out what was left in the cooler, a bit more egg

salad and some juice, and placed the trout in there. I looked at
the grandparents again. The man was rubbing lotion onto his
wife's back, first warming the cream in his large hands. She
faced the water. I imagined a series of numbers tattooed into his
right hand, small and blurred with age against his white skin.

My mother sat in the shade of the parasol. She was flipping
through a magazine with Ruby, the one she always had lying
around, *Pattern and Design*, pointing out the dresses and
sweaters she wanted to make for her for the fall. Monika was
still in the sun. She was working on the last of the wine from
lunch. After the fish went into the icebox she'd stretched out
straight on her back. With a twinge I found the line of sweat in
the slight crease of her abdomen.

"The wind's good, Peter," my father said. "What do you say?"

I grabbed my shirt and we started for the stairwell. But my
heart sank when I heard Günter's rushed footsteps coming up
behind us in the parking lot. I wanted my father to say something, that there wouldn't be enough room in the sailboat,
which wouldn't have been stretching the truth that much. But
I knew he wouldn't. Maybe he thought Uncle Günter was coming around. Maybe he was snapping out of it because they were
leaving soon.

My father put down the deposit and left his credit card with
the man at the desk. We got number forty-five, a blue, two-man
Laser. Although I knew there would be no problem with three
people, I wanted the man at the desk to say that one of us would
have to sit it out. New regulations on crowding. Even if it was
me. But he only nodded his head and smiled. He helped my
uncle and my father lift the boat off the racks. They carried it
over the gravel driveway and nosed it into the lake. I followed
behind with the life jackets and tossed them into the cockpit.

"We'll see what we can do today," my father said once we got
started. We began slowly, cutting through the water, tacking our
way out of the shallow bay. There were other boats in the middle of the lake, small, no other blue ones except ours, different
colours cutting across the water like coloured shark fins. As we
made our way to tap into the stream of wind that swept across
the middle of the lake I noticed that Günter wasn't comfortable

out here. In the sailboat or on the water, I couldn't tell. But I knew right off that he didn't know anything about sailing. I remembered that he hadn't come swimming with the rest of us. But he followed my father's instructions, where to sit, how to move with the boat. He tried to show interest by asking after the boat's mechanics, pointing to the jib and boom and knocking his knuckles against the top of the centreboard. I wondered why he was out with us, why he'd come.

Once we got to the middle of the lake I saw Günter was nervous, that he needed to sit quietly for a while and get his bearings. My father was at the tiller, the mainsheet in his left hand. I was at the bow. I liked sailing, I knew how, but it was my father's love and I never insisted on taking over the reins. Anything to do with water was my father's love, and I wondered at how terrible it was that it should kill his mother the way it had. He offered me the tiller a couple of times before we got out to open water, but I was happy to sit up at the bow and watch him work the boat. He was relaxed and smiling, talking loudly against the wind. He'd told me stories about winning this and that cup when he was a kid, when he sailed competitively for big prizes on lakes with wonderful names like Ammersee and Konigsee, all mysterious mountain lakes in Bavaria, close to Italy.

He pulled us in as close to shore as we could get without crossing the buoys that marked off the swimmers' area to make a pass by Monika, Ruby, and my mother. We waved until they saw us, and Ruby stood and jumped up and down and cupped her hands around her mouth and called out. I didn't hear anything but a distant, high screech. Monika hoisted her wine glass above her head and held it there like the Statue of Liberty. We jumped over some small water as we veered full and by out to the middle of the lake. I dragged my hand under the waves, watching my fingers turn pale yellow and then dark like a fish. I looked up. My hair blew around my face. Günter was smiling now. They were talking back and forth in German, but I could only hear the ghosts of their voices because of the sail flapping against the wind. The gold medal count, my fish, our empty swimming pool, my uncle, even Monika, were all gone now. The feeling of jumping over the water, watching people speed by in the other sailboats, red and yellow with small suns stitched into their sails, waving to them as we sped by. The air was hot, even with the wind on us and the misting spray coming up off the bow.

As we approached the end of the lake where I'd caught my fish, I pointed to the inlet to show my father and he suddenly, unexpectedly tacked to starboard and I went over the side. I didn't have my life preserver on. I saw the yellow-black rocks come up quick against me, was stunned into sinking because I thought I was still pointing towards the inlet about to say "Trout heaven, full steam ahead" but I couldn't because my mouth was spreading with lake water and I was sinking, had no idea where I was. The thought of my grandmother washed over my eyes, how she must have seen the same thing, weeds and rocks, pulled under by the weight of her orange wedding dress, cloaked in water. I felt, saw a hand on my shoulder, large and scaly, descend from above and grab me by my right arm and pull me back to the surface. Into air. I breathed. It pulled me up and laid me across the side of the boat. The sail had dropped. I felt us stopped dead in the water and I started hacking up skunky water from my lungs, spitting up over the edge of the boat. I turned my face up to the sail's small stitched sun and found my uncle looking over me, his entire upper body black from the water, his hair dripping, my father's face white, terrified as it had been the day his mother disappeared into the Trent-Severn Waterway the day of her second wedding. Holding fast the tiller, stopped dead in the water. Saved by my uncle, the plasterer.

I was okay by the time we got home late that afternoon. I'd sunk. I'd swallowed some water, that was it. Günter saved my life and my father came close to seeing his son drown a year after his own mother. But only almost; that was it. Nothing happened, I told myself. I sat in the back seat on the way home, my hand on my father's shoulder the whole way. He'd told my mother, but down-played the accident. She knew I'd fallen in, I'd gotten wet. I told her I'd had my life jacket on. Günter. I owed him one. China hadn't won a single medal so far. But in their culture, I knew my life was his now.

Over the next two days Ruby and I circled the pool as our uncle worked, so expectant that we forgot about the Games entirely. Günter finished the job two days before my birthday, three days before they were to catch their plane back to Munich. The blue paint he'd finished with needed twenty-four hours to dry. I counted on the clock exactly when I could turn on the hose, desperate for water in my own back yard. I was counting on an Indian summer. It was already September. Ruby and I were going back to school next week. My father had said it didn't make sense filling the pool this time of year. I knew he was right when he told me that, at best, we'd only get a couple of weeks' use out of it. It wouldn't be worth the chemicals we'd have to pour in. I played up the fact that my birthday was in a few days, that I'd never had a party without a swim in the pool. It was a family tradition, I said. But I also knew he wanted to see if all the work Uncle Günter had put in down there had paid off, all the waiting.

I turned on the hose the night before I turned fifteen. The pool was half full by morning. That afternoon we prepared my trout on the barbecue. We'd cleaned them and put them in the freezer because nobody had felt like cooking the night we got home from the lake. We ate hamburgers along with the fish and, for dessert, a chocolate cake that Ruby had helped my mother make. Fifteen blue and red candles sticking out the top. I made a wish and blew once as hard as I could. The flames lowered like sails under a hard wind, tipped, and drowned in the white icing, but one remained upright. I licked my finger and thumb, prepared to snuff it out, but Günter quickly leaned over the table and blew it down.

After lunch, around mid-afternoon, we staged our own Olympics. Ruby and I got our bathing suits on. Our somersaults over the grass that afternoon were as high as they had ever been. Monika called out scores along with my parents while Uncle Günter sat and watched. On my hands I walked from the rose bushes to the deck, up onto the diving board, waited a moment, savouring, and slid smoothly, finally, into the cold water. The pool reached around my body like an animal, squeezed me into a tight ball and, for a moment, quickly, my grandmother came back to me, the rocks I'd seen at the bottom of the lake rising. I remembered her down there, the way she must have spent her last conscious seconds before she passed out. I opened my eyes and saw the faint traces of my uncle's repairs crawling up the sloping sides like the vines of underwater flowers, her face among them, tangled and smiling.

I came to the surface, breathed self-consciously, and dared Ruby to jump in. "You'll get used to it," I told her, splashing outwards with an open palm. She stood on the diving board, a game of ours from the summer before, playing it up for the adults as they sat at the picnic table, drinking their coffee and peach schnapps. She stepped back, took a running jump, and arced through the air, hung against the real sun, my little sister, the future gymnast, and broke the water with a delighted screech. Monika smiled and raised her glass over her head. From the water I saw my uncle leave the picnic table.

After dinner we turned on the TV for the first time in two days. So far Canada had only won three bronze and a silver. We were hoping for news of gold. The Games were closing soon. We didn't have much time. At nine o'clock we settled in the TV room to watch the day's highlights, Ruby in the beanbag, my mother with her knitting, my father leafing through *Wind and Sail*. News footage lit up the room. There was a shot of an airport, then masked men and helicopters. Monika was sitting in the rocking chair beside Ruby. Uncle Günter came in from the front porch, where he'd been sitting with his back against a pillar, reading a copy of *Stern* since dinner. I made a space for him on the couch. I felt the heat come off him when his thigh touched mine.

"You're from there," Ruby said, grabbing Monika's hand when she heard the voice-over say Fürstenfeldbruck. The announcer said the Munich Olympiad had been suspended today at three-forty-five. The Israeli team was withdrawing. Günter leaned forward. The magazine rolled in his hand. There was a shot of flags flying at half mast. His eyes rolled back into his head like they'd done the day he inhaled the dry dusty earth of my mother's garden. Then the voice-over again. Eleven

Israelis killed, one Munich sergeant, five terrorists. My mother's hands fell open. Then we saw the pictures of stockinged faces peering around corners, guns in the air. As we watched she translated for her brother, her voice floating beneath the glow of the screen. Günter's face didn't change. Ruby didn't understand what they were talking about. "What does hostage mean? What's *hostage!*"

"Prisoner," I said. Then the footage of men in masks, a man throwing a hand grenade into a helicopter as it sat on the tarmac, its still propellers hanging low to the ground like the branches of the elm tree I'd stood under while watching Monika. There was a moment's pause. Then it exploded like in the movies. The room filled with the same drowning yellow rays of sun I'd seen at the lake before my uncle's arm pulled me back to the surface, came off the helicopter's black and white explosion.

"Okay, that's enough," my mother said angrily, rolling the ball of wool from her lap. She put down her knitting needles, took Ruby by the wrist, and led her upstairs. "I don't *want* to be a hostage," I heard her say as she stomped her feet up the stairs beside my mother. "Don't *you* treat me like a hostage!" My mother came back down a few minutes later. She didn't say anything. I'd been allowed to stay. It was my birthday.

"*Juden!*" Günter said then with a smile on his face. He rolled his fish eyes back around from the inside of his head towards me, as if I was to understand something that no one else could. He laughed something in German I didn't understand and slapped the rolled-up magazine down against my thigh. My mother shot her head around to him, looked at him icily. Didn't he own me now? I thought. Rocks came up at me, my lungs filling. His hand was warm on my leg. My father put his hands on his knees, about to step between them, his wife and his brother-in-law. Monika was ready to speak. Then I saw something in her eyes that told me this was between brothers and sisters. Not husbands and wives. Not Israelis and Germans and Palestinians. This was about the salt that had pervaded their lives, drained the life from their father, kept the scent of death from the door that June in 1944. About cattle cars and blizzards. It was about the heart of my family. Monika was not blood. She would have her turn at him upstairs, alone. Somewhere else. Not here. Speak to him for the first time in weeks, maybe years. But my mother got up and left the room. I heard the door to her knitting room close behind her upstairs. Then Monika left the room and walked out onto the porch. I saw her through the front window. She leaned into a rose that clung to the trellis, a darker hole in the night grid, and her chest filled. My father turned off the TV and led me upstairs to bed. From my room I heard him across the hall with my mother, speaking softly. I imagined Ruby lying in bed, drawing the word *hostage* in the air with a finger. The vacation was over. Tomorrow, they'd be gone.

After everyone had gone to bed, I got up to pee. I stood over the sound of spilling water, still half asleep, and remembered what my uncle was leaving behind for us – a full pool, a wound in the earth shining in the moonlight. I went downstairs, through the kitchen and into the dark sunroom that opened onto the back yard, and found Günter in the pool. From the door, I watched him swim, his long arms powering him through the water, back and forth like a man pacing the length of a small room. I walked out onto the damp grass and crouched in the shadows by the rock garden. For an hour and more I waited like that, expecting him to go under. I pulled a piece of crab grass from the lawn and sucked on it while I watched his darkened figure move through the water. Then I felt the first drop of rain to fall in eight weeks, a light sprinkle, and now the sky swirled and it began to pour. The pool jumped alive and bubbled. I stabbed my tongue into the warm rain, savouring the end of our drought, and formed a cup with my hands. I heard Günter call out to me. But I didn't answer. What if he'd passed something on to me? I thought. What if, at the lake, my life had passed into his hands when he pulled me from the water? And again, through the rain, he called out to me. I listened, waiting, afraid to answer, then raised my cupped hands to my lips and drank.

TERRY GRIGGS

Momma Had a Baby

*A*nd her head popped off. My cousin Nile had spread himself out on the lawn, lethal as any chemical, and was decapitating dandelions with his thumbnail. Flicked sunheads spun haywire this way and that, ditsy blondes. *Momma had a baby* (pause) *and her head popped off* (flick). Another (flick) and another (flick). If the dandelions had been further along, he'd be blowing them bare, infesting everyone's lawns with his wishes, banks of yellow gold erupting days later, the flower of his desire for biceps, for cool cash, maybe a call from the Leafs' manager. ("Look, Keon's injured. We *need* you!") As far as nature was concerned, Nile was better than dogs' hindquarters, pantlegs, and wind put together. Restless in fields, unwashed, he went about her pollinating business like a pimp. I felt for Nile the same degree of relatedness one might feel for a nightcrawler – a cousinage that had more to do with inhabiting the same stretch of earth than sharing anything as intimate as genetic material. But, twelve years old, with an undescended testicle, Nile was the love interest, take it or leave it.

Inside was estrogen city, all women, mostly related, the air fibrous with connection. And even the few who weren't blood knew each other inside out, friends and neighbours who were practically sewn together, chain stitched, with their knowledge and informed speculation about one another. Only one person stood on the edge of this dense familiarity like someone having an out-of-body experience, and that was a woman who'd recently moved here from some smug Southern Ontario town, and appeared to have her jaw rusted shut. She was remembering, was all. A younger sister who had succumbed to scarlet fever at the age of fifteen had arrived unbidden in her head and now after all these years rode there like a conquering whip-snapping queen in a chariot. Naturally, this gave her a somewhat self-absorbed expression.

Anyway, they were all packed into Auntie Viv's living room for a last-minute, hold-your-breath baby shower. Very last-minute, time stretched tight as a drum over Mother's huge belly. She was two weeks late and Auntie Viv thought this little party might break the monotony, if not the water. Mother hoped not, her water that is, for she was beached on Viv's newly uphol-stered chesterfield, formerly a spirit-lowering beige and brown tweed, now red and slick as an internal organ, enough colour and texture to make you giddy. Viv had put up bilious fleshy drapes to match, and Mother figured this show-off reason was the real one for the shower, not her.

A fountain of dandelion heads spraying up outside past the window caught Mother's attention. *The Birth of Venus*, she thought, even though she had only ever seen a commercial ver-sion of that famous painting, a picture in a magazine advertising shampoo. Still, wouldn't it be lovely, a fresh-water baby rising out of the lake on a clamshell, dandelion heads flocking the feathery-soft air? So beautiful, so easy. Mother was terrified of dying in childbirth, and understood her fear to be a restraining band, wide as a strop, holding her baby back. She entertained a morbid notion that already she had marked the baby, that it would be reticent and fearful all its life, and she prayed it would find a source of courage somewhere deep inside itself. If she lived, she resolved to call her baby Hero, boy or girl. If she died, Morie would call it Stu if it was a boy, and Sue if it was a girl. That being the extent of it, Mother vowed to hold out at least until the naming formalities were concluded.

For her part, Auntie Viv was more than curious to see this baby, on account of Mother simultaneously losing her virginity and committing adultery scarcely hours into her marriage. She probably set some sort of record for the town, though it's not the kind of accomplishment you'd want to print up. Might be printed on the baby's face, mind you: Cousin Tony's visage appearing clear and crisp as a photograph, reproductive values more conclusive than the Shroud of Turin. This notion tickled Auntie Viv, for she considered her sister-in-law to be simpy and shallow as a pool. Piously nice. Let Mother pretend otherwise but marriage had corrupted her, the cracks were beginning to show. Auntie Viv smiled her fox smile and wrenched her push-up bra back into place. Damn thing was chomping on her ribs *just like* something invented by a man.

When you think Viv had only cooked up this shower idea the day before, Mother was getting a pretty good haul. Not that she needed more sleepers in neuter green and yellow – no one willing to commit her firm opinions as to the baby's sex in material terms – or teeny tiny vests (already outgrown) that made the whole assembly chant *Awwwww* when she held them up for ritual gift inspection and approval. And, since this *was* her fifth shower to date, she had enough fuzzy blankets and quilts at home to bury the kid alive. Most of those present had contributed plenty to the prospective infant, dearly hoping that at this rate they weren't going to have to fork out for its education, too.

My grandmother, Albertha Pinkham, veteran of all five, knew enough to bring her gift in instalments. So far, the oddly shaped packages wrapped in brown paper and stuck with adhesive contained wooden slats, spindles, rockers, and a seat. She promised to knock the rocking chair together and paint it once she had the squalling evidence in her large sliver-flecked hands. Albertha had ironed her linen dress for the first shower, gesture enough she felt, and now it was so wrinkled it might have been in pain. Gruesome. A sartorial senescence mimicking her own decline. She bowed her head and dropped a brief prayer into the creases along the lines of *No stupid games, okay? And do You think we could get on with the show here?* By show, she did not mean more teething rings and baby wipes, but contractions, a crescendo of them, sudden and strong, a muscular fanfare announcing the arrival of. . . . Glancing over at her child, stranded on Viv's hideous sofa, a giant's collapsed kidney, she recognized that aura of fear, Mother's stricken look, like that of an animal about to be clubbed. Albertha tacked a stern post-script onto her prayer: *Remember, I go first. Don't mess up.* How far afield had those rumours about her daughter's infidelity actually drifted? Divine punishment? Well really, grandbabies weren't so thick on the ground around here that anyone, divine or otherwise, should gripe if one came swaddled in a story or two. What was life without embroidery, anyway? Coarse cotton, that's all. Plain as unsullied paper, too plain for words.

Momma had a baby . . .

"What *is* that noise I keep hearing?"

"Nile, that lunk. Out on the grass."

and her head popped off.

Death, you know, crashing the party, mute as a shadow falling through the window. The uninvited guest. Which isn't exactly true, for my other grandmother, Gramma Young, had been issuing special invitations for years, beaming signals into the black depths of space, courting that one polygamous alien, violent lover, terminal seducer. Thus far she was unrequited, and a regular menace on the subject.

"My *last* shower," she sighed, sailing this hoary news across the room.

As her foreboding announcement was the very one she had made at the other four showers, no one was buying it. Any sympathies aroused had already been slashed to the bone.

"Mine too. We're *all* hoping that."

"Pine. A rough pine box, nothin' fancy for me."

"Chin up, Gramma. This is supposed to be a happy occasion. Think, real soon there'll be a new baby to cuddle."

"I'll never see it."

"C'mon, none of that talk now."

"New life comes into the world, old life's booted out."

"Amen, and praise the Lord!" said Auntie Viv, who'd been sneaking swigs from one of the flower vases she kept topped up with gin. The longevity of Viv's birthday roses always amazed Uncle Clyde, a phenomenon he could only attribute to some secret source of power generated by Viv herself.

"Tastes like soap." Gramma Young was chewing with athletic effort one of Batty Pock's shortbread squares.

Instantly, a message written in apologetic smiles, a kind of facial shorthand, was flashed to Batty that said, *Never mind her, the old coot.*

Batty shifted uncomfortably in her chair. Whatever did happen to that soap powder, the box sitting on the counter when she was searching for the extra flour?

"*Mother,*" warned Aunt Faith, seizing any opportunity to pay Gramma back, coin for coin, for every admonishing word she'd received as a child. Faith was the snappy sister, my least favourite aunt. She had resentment the way some people have religion – visibly – she wore it like a prow. If feeling slighted, overworked, neglected, she would take her husband Earl apart molecule by molecule, then reassemble him, a lesser man. She was Nile's mother, and he her son, and they fit together like a mathematical problem you could work on most of your life and never figure out.

Drop dead, Gramma was about to retort – she absolutely refused to let Faith have the last word – when, unaccountably, it *was* and she *did.* Drop dead. But the drop was so slight, gentle as ash drifting down, it was as if a quieting finger had been placed lovingly on her heart to untrouble its agitated and relentless motion. Indeed, Gramma had cried wolf for so long that her death was as tame and friendly as a panting, tail-thumping companion lolling at her feet. *I rest my case,* her body finally said, and in such an understated, such a gracious and accomplished manner, that no one, not even she, noticed her passing. She sat very, very still, and said nothing further.

Minnie Evans screamed, a startled little product, but it was only at Nile, who had smushed his face up against the window. Give him six years and he might almost resemble James Dean, but at the moment, features flatly pressed into the glass, he could have easily passed for a package of plastic-wrapped chicken thighs from the Red & White.

An intuitive awareness of something amiss perhaps sparked the inevitable birthing stories. Ancient Mariners all, women trotted out their individual traumas, sparing Mother nothing in the way of still births, haemorrhages, caesarean sections, and marathon labours. Babies' shrill kitten cries repeatedly stabbed the air, and gallons of lost, fictional, and phantom blood sloshed through the room.

My girl cousin, Amy, who had made a bow-hat out of an upturned tinfoil plate and the discarded gift bows, rose as if on a wave of this unsettling talk and placed it on Gramma Young's head. Her festive and improvisational bit of haberdashery slipped, caught on a stiff curl, and came to rest at a rakish and merry angle.

"She's dead," said the woman from the south who had not yet uttered a single word. At least she spent her embarrassed verbal fund well. It was to the point.

"Pardon?" someone asked.

"What?"

"Oh God, look at Gramma Young."

"My arse," said Auntie Viv, "stick a pin in her."

"Oh my God."

"She's only asleep."

"Faking it."

"No. No, I don't think so."

"Give her a little push, Minnie."

"Not *me*."

"Heavens," said Albertha, reaching out to give Eve Young a wakening nudge, this *other* grandmother to whom she had rarely ever spoken, certainly nothing beyond courtesies. If you could call a grunt a courtesy. Truth was she didn't have time for whiners, and now she realized, touch telling no lie, that Eve didn't have time at all, it had withdrawn itself from her, its animating caress, its ticking breath.

They all shivered and stared at one another.

"I'll call Glanville, why don't I?" This was Marion Goodwin, the undertaker's wife. Marion usually managed to appal and fascinate in about equal measure. What *was* it like being married to the Gland Man was a question that swam up from a depth and circled visibly close to the surface. Imagine his unearthly cold hands reaching for you in bed at night (sheets reeking of formaldehyde), hands fat and grub-white that only hours before had been palpating the internal organs of corpses, drawing blood out of bodies with the same ease and indifference with which they might drain Freshie out of coolers at a picnic.

Marion wrote poetry, verse boxes that never seemed to contain humans, but heavily featured dewdrops, sunsets, and an array of symbols inert as stone markers. These she published in the local paper. *More embalmed mots*, the editor would groan when he saw her approaching down the walk, clutching yet another torso-thick bundle of paper in her arms, that unnerving pink smile of hers indelibly printed on her face.

"Viv," ordered Albertha, "call the ambulance."

"Hey," said Viv, as she sashayed out of the room, "I've just thought up a great name for a female comedy group." She stuck her head back in to deliver the punchline. "Titters."

An outbreak of giggles erupted and was quickly suppressed.

"Viv's in shock," said someone, kindly.

Someone else began to whimper, very quietly.

By this time Nile had taken off, pelting away like a hunted man. Soon he'd be tearing through fields, running and running, long grass singing past.

"It's coming," said Mother.

"So's Christmas," snapped Minnie Evans. A novice to the potency of sarcasm, she promptly fell apart weeping buckets.

"What is, dear? The ambulance?"

"Already? Alec won't set out on a run 'til he's had a coffee and a smoke."

"The baby," Mother whispered. This a mumbled, prayer-faint revelation that was indeed underlined by Alec's keening flashing progress down our street.

"What baby?" demanded Aunt Faith.

Then a single dawning *Oh!* of recollection was all it took for everyone to fly into action. Mother was rescued from Viv's sofa by a dozen pair of hands, bundled into a shawl warm as a nest, and delivered with midwifely solicitations and endearments to the ambulance revving its engine at the door.

One thing you have to say for it, the trip to the hospital was cost efficient. Not only did Mother, thrown suddenly into wracking convulsive labour, have to share the ambulance with

Gramma Young, cooling rapidly and inviting no intimacies, but Alec stopped at the Perdues' place halfway there to pick up pie-padded Horace and wedge him in as well. Horace had swallowed his pencil stub while working on a crossword. "*Women,*" he confided to the male-grey upholstery into which his face was pressed. You had to wonder if that was the word he'd choked on filling in the puzzle, or whether he considered his emergency eclipsed by the usual female problems. Women, there was no escaping them.

And to prove it, I added my weight to the world. Nine pounds, fifteen ounces of pure solid self. Mere minutes after they wheeled Mother into the delivery room, some intern had me by the heels. Well. My first bat's-eye view of the situation was not consoling. The room swung muzzy, as though rubbed in grease. Mother lay bloody and limp, a brutalized body cast aside. Pain seared my backside (never trust a doctor), and I let go a river of sound, my tongue a flailing, undisciplined instrument. But I must have known even then, grabbing at the air (I had Albertha's hands!), that the power would eventually be mine to carve that river into the precise and commanding language I needed. For the present, raw underspeech. I said: *Mother, don't leave me.* I said: *Nile, get your balls in order, boy, your Hero's come to town.*

SASENARINE PERSAUD

Canada Geese and Apple Chatney

Bai dhem time something else – rough – rough like rass. And was no laughter. Yuh want hear about dhem time? Leh me tell yuh. And don't bother with Writerji. He's mih friend but remember he's a writer. He change-up everything, mix-up people and place so nobady could tell who is who, and what what. And if yuh ain't know, all sound like true. But dhat is because Writerji good. Well he always good. Yuh see dhat story about running from immigration officer which set in New York. Dhat same thing happen here in Toronto to he. And was he, me, and Hermit sharing a apartment at the same time. Yuh know how Anand get dhat name Writerji? Is me give he, me and Hermit. Ask Hermit when yuh see he.

And dhat bai Hermit is something else. A holiday – was Christmas. Just the three ah we in the apartment. Snow like ass outside. Prem and Kishore invite we over but Hermit old car ain't starting, and anyway too much snow. And Prem and Kishore ain't gat car – dhey living in the east end, somewhere behind gaad back near Morningside. In dhem days, once people know yuh illegal, nobady want see yuh, nobady invite yuh at them house. Even yuh own relative – people come hey and change. Money, money, money. Mih own uncle don't call me. And when he ass going to UG he staying at we place, five years – mih mother neva tek a cent from he. When yuh illegal every-bady think yuh want money, or something. Yuh don't let peo-ple know you situation – yuh laugh outside. So is just dhe three a we. Snow tearing tail and we putting lash on some Johnnie Walker Black Label. Hermit bring out he big tape and we playing some Mukesh and Rafi. Suddenly the tape finish. Is a eerie silence. Fat snow flakes khat khat khat on dhe window pane.

Suddenly Hermit seh, "And Writerji – a hope yuh ain't turn out like Naipaul. Yuh see how he write *Miguel Street* and *Biswas*. Mek a mockery a everybady, mek a mockery a dhe culture . . ."

"Ah, come on, Hermit. Naipaul nat so bad. He write fiction, stories. And stories are more than just the truth, more than just a little lie. And we more critical than Naipaul. Remember how we say dhat all pandit ah bandit! What more derogatory than that."

"But we say it as joke!"

"Same thing with Naipaul!"

"Anyway, mek sure yuh ass don't write nothing about me."

"He gat to write about something, Hermit," I teasing Hermit, "and what you gun do if he write about you?" Since Guyana we calling he Hermit because he like a bookworm, always reading when yuh miss he. Was dhe same thing here. When he come home and after he eat, he head straight fuh he room and read. Sometimes he look TV with we.

"Well, we friends a lang time, since high school, but don't do dhis to me. I serious. Don't let me recognize anything about me." Man is like dhe cold come inside the apartment. Hermit serious, real serious. Rare thing for Hermit. Since I come to Toronto, only one time I see he so serious and angry. I tell you, dhem quiet people, yuh could neva tell. Funny how we always teasing he about he hook nose and he long hair since school days. Anybady with a joke about finding anything, is Hermit nose could find it. Anybady want string to tie anything, is Hermit hair. Talk about bird, is description by length and curve of beak – like Hermit beak-nose. When yuh can't find anybady – dhey gaan into seclusion like Hermit. But Hermit always laugh. Dhis time Hermit serious.

That other time was a month or two before. We gaan up Jane Street to see Hetram but Hetram ain't home yet. So Hermit seh

let we say go across to the Jane-Finch Mall at dhe McDonald's.
Buy coffee and some chicken burger or something – he paying –
and check out the girls. Funny thing about Hermit was he like
spend a lat a time by heself but when he come outside is like he
can't get enough of people, place, things. And he pleasant and
outgoing. If a nice chick pass, Hermit lose shyness. He gan
straight up to she and tell she she nice, sometimes mek a date
with she or something. Was a Sunday and dhe mall full because
of the flea market. McDonald's full too. So Writerji and me go
and hold a table while Hermit in the line. Me and Writerji sur-
veying everybady else. Suddenly a little commotion start up
before the cashier. Hermit and a dread squaring off. Me and
Writerji run up.

"Listen, man. I'm in this line before you. Yuh just want to
come from nowhere and get infront me!" Hermit voice not loud
but like a spring, one hand in he jacket pocket. Well, yuh know
Jane-Finch area. Plenty West Indians, plenty Jamaicans with
dhey drugs and crime and bullying people like dhey own dhe
whole place. We think Hermit holding he wallet because of
pickpocket.

"Listen – I gettin serve now, coolie bai."

"Not before me, *rass*-ta." Hermit deliberately breaking up
the word. The dread black like tar and about four inches taller
than Hermit, long dreadlocks and one a dhem green and red
cap with Selassie picture. Hermit about 5' 9", not exactly short,
he hair long like a yogi, and he skin fair. A odd contrast and
similarity.

"I gettin serve now or is shooting."

"Not before me, *rass*-ta." Hermit turning squarely to dhe
dread and straightening and suddenly smiling, "friend I is a
peaceful man – like Gandhi – you know Gandhi. Believe in non-
violence. But lil advice from me; when yuh talk about shooting
yuh should gat a gun in yuh hand first. I know people – nat me –
who would shoot yuh dhe moment yuh talk about shooting. I
know people – nat me – who would shoot yuh cunt dead, now, if
yuh talk another word." I getting coldsweat hearing Hermit. He
ain't afraid though, he smiling. And I thinking, praying that the
dread and he partner ain't start shooting fuh truth. I think we

dead. Well, is Jane-Finch Mall and a whole crowd a Jamaicans suddenly stan up behind dhe dread. Just Hermit and me and Writerji near he. Dhem Indians and white people stay right at dhem table like sheep. Everything happening like lightning.

"Next cashier open here," a supervisor said, smiling and breaking the tension. "May I help you here, sir," she said pleasantly. She just open a cashier near the dread. Nothing like a pretty white girl to disarm a dread! Dread turn to she with a swagger and smiling like Hermit ain't exist. Later when we in the car driving home Writerji burst out, "Hermit, I think we dead, man. Nearly piss mih pants."

"Nah. He just bluffing."

"What if he tek out a gun?" I ask.

"If he only put he hand in he coat pocket, I woulda shoot dhe bitch. An he know it."

"With what?"

"This." Hermit reach into he jacket and tek out a small blue automatic gun.

"Yuh mean yuh holding that thing all dhe time? How lang yuh gat this, man!" Writerji tek the gun and examine it fine fine.

"When I first come to this country." Man, I in shock. I live with Hermit for six months and neva know this. But Hermit in Canada six years before me. And he live in Montreal most a dhe time. Same time I come from Georgetown, same time he come down from Montreal. Dhem Frenchie racial, he seh, and dhem want dhem own country. Like if dhem own anything. Is thief, they thief dhe land from dhem Amerindians – and don't matter Frenchie lose dhe 1980 referendum. Next time round and next time. Toronto tame compared to Montreal. . . .

Well, me and Writerji remember this incident and the gun same time, and how Hermit cool like cucumber and scared a nobady. Suddenly Writerji smile. "Hermit – relax, my friend. Ah know yuh hungry. Well, this meat defrost. I will cook some – curry?"

"Nah, how about some bunjal geese," Hermit laughed, "and a bake one – come, I'll come and help you. Put on dhat Sundar-Popo tape, Jones." Hermit turn to me a bit unsteady. He nicknamed me Jones because I see Jim Jones when he first land in

Guyana, and because I went and see he fraud miracle in Sacred Heart Church lang before all them murders. Well, I start one big laugh. And Hermit start laughing too.

I tell yuh, times was tough. Hermit just come down from Montreal – he just get he landed and want make a new start – he give too many false name and false social insurance number in Montreal, and dhem Frenchie getting more racial – I coming up from GT and illegal, then baps, Writerji landing down on we. See how things happen! Remember dhem time when government thugs try to break up we meeting at Kitty Market Square and dhey get beat up and run in the police station for help. Was me, Cuffy and Akkara, and some other bais from Buxton. They shoot Akkara in dhe gardens and seh he had gun fuh overthrow dhe government, and dhey beat up Cuffy in he garage and put a AK-47 in he car trunk and seh he about to resist arrest, that he commit suicide in jail. All this just after Rodney assassination. Well, I ain't wait around. Them days yuh didn't had to get visa to come to Canada. Next flight I in Toronto. But mih uncle and he wife meking all sort a remark. If I bathe two times a day – that was a summer hotter than anything in Guyana – they complaining I bathe too lang and too often, I go to the toilet too often – is money water cost. This nat Guyana! Yuh pay fuh water here! Well, a meet Hermit in Knob Hill Farms one day and he seh he gat same prablem, he went through same thing – leh we rent a two-bedroom. I ain't gat no wuk yet, you know. He seh, man, no prablem. He get a social insurance number and a name fuh mih. Some Indian name. The man dead and one a Hermit girlfriend get the name and number. Frank Sharma. See how Frank stick. All yuh must be think that I change mih name, become Frank instead of Ramesh because I want become Canadian duck. Nah. This coolie ain't shame he name. Anyway I Frank Sharma now. And frighten like ass when I go any place to wuk and I gat to say I name Frank Sharma. I trembling but trying to look bold, hoping I ain't say meh real name.

Yuh think is three cents we go though! Well, I ain't gat no wuk yet and Hermit just pick up a thing in a factory. Although he just get he landed, money still small. Almost a month and I ain't get nothing, then I walk in a factory at Steeles and Bathurst desperate – and get tek on. The supervisor want a forklift operator. Man, I neva drive a donkey-cart yet, muchless forklift. I tell the man, with experience, I could manage dhe forklift, anything. Lucky for me the forklift break down, and the forklift driver who didn't show up, turn up next day. The supervisor find wuk for me packing boxes. And next two weeks, bam, Writerji turn up in the apartment lobby. He dhe last man to land in Canada before Canadian immigration decide yuh gat to get visa from Guyana, too much Guyanese fulling up Toronto. We bunking on dhe ground, can't afford a bed or even mattress, in a room and squeezing cents. Hermit trying to get a name and number for Writerji.

Well, Writerji waiting fuh he name and number but he ain't wasting time. He want learn about Toronto and Canada. He find library and reading up about Canada, about trees and birds. Whenever we go out anyway he pointing out birch, spruce, oak, cedar, weeping willow, pussy willow, ash, he pointing out bluejay, redstart, sparrow, starling, cardinal. He teking walk in park – yuh want know which park? Is at Eglinton and Jane street – Eglinton Flats. Autumn coming and Writerji want experience Canadian fall – colours radiant over all dhem trees. Geese coming in to land sweet sweet like plane. Every afternoon he coming home and writing poems. A night he writing a poem and suddenly he buss out one big laugh. He seh we thinking money scarce and cutting we tail and food all over dhe place. All them geese nice and fat, heading south fuh winter. He seh if is Guyana yuh think all them duck could deh so nice and lazy all over dhe place, preening themself like majesty and nobady own them, and people starving? And other people feeding them bread and fattening them up fuh we!

He seh why we don't catch some a dhem geese and stock up for winter. Them geese heading south to get away from the cold and now is dhe right time. And he tell we how in England dhem bai do dhe same thing and some Trini writer name Selvon write about this thing in a book call *Lonely Londoners*. Hermit remember he hear this someway but he laugh and seh nobady neva write this – and how he know? Tell yuh the truth, I see them geese and I thinking same thing – how dhem bais in Guyana woulda done wuk them down.

"Is how I know? I'm a writer man!"

"So Hermit is Gandhi like Gandhiji and yuh is Writer – like Writerji," I buss out one laugh.

Well, Hermit still ain't believe that this thing write down, so Writerji and we gone to St. Dennis library near Weston Road and Eglinton corner and he get Hermit to borrow *The Lonely Londoners* and *Ways of Sunlight* by Sam Selvon. As soon as we get home he find the page and start read how hunger washing Cap tail and Cap decided to ketch seagull and eat them. We laugh good. And dhat is how he get dhe name Writerji. From dhat night we call he Writerji. But he done plan this thing. We could buy expire bread, and night time head down to Eglinton Flats Park. Them geese sleeping right next to a little culvert and all over the grass behind them trees. Two a-we could catch ducks and one man swipe dhe neck. Hermit get excited. He want try this thing. Well, is me and Hermit end up catching all them ducks and geese. I holding them and Hermit swiping them neck. All Writerji doing is holding bag and keeping look-out. Just like he since schooldays. He always thinking up some-thing and me and Hermit doing the wuk. A trunk full a ducks in large double garbage bags. We skin them when we get home. Writerji saying we ain't stupid like Cap and we dispose of them feathers and skin real good. Nobody could catch we. Well them geese taste good.

Hermit seh next weekend let we take some fuh Prem and Kishore. They apartment overlooking Morningside Park and them maple trees flaming with colours. Writerji want tek a walk in the park and see this thing near. I want see too – was mih first autumn – but I playing I ain't care before them bai start laugh at me and call me Newfie and Pole and Balgobin-come-to-town. Writerji ain't care about who laugh he, he want see this thing close, hold them leaves. So we laughing he, asking if he really want size up more geese because it gat geese in that park. We teking a drink on a picnic table in the park and Writerji disap-pear. Next thing he coming back with he hand full a them small sour apple. He can't believe all them apple falling on the grass and wasting. People wasteful in Canada, he muttering over and over. Writerji want help to pick some nice green apple on them tree. Why? He thinking just like how yuh use green mango, or bilimbi, or barahar to make achaar and chatney, why not green apple. And right then mango scarce in Toronto, cost a fortune. Them days was not like nowadays when you gat West Indian store every corner. Them days you only get fruits from the West Indies when anybody coming. But that apple chatney taste good with them geese we bring for Prem and Kishore. Writerji didn't make no chatney though. He gat all dhem ideas but is me, Hermit, and Prem and Kishore in they apartment making apple chatney! Not three cents dhat bai Writerji.

Anyway just after new year Hermit get a number for Writerji and same time a Vietnamese girl get pregnant and quit. So I talk to dhe boss and Writerji get tek on. Well, is a factory making knockdown cardboard cartons up in Concorde by Steeles and Bathurst and is winter. We getting up five in the morning to reach for seven. Writerji get easy job. How he manage I ain't know. See, I working on line. As fast as them boxes come off the line we gat to pack them on a crate. Yuh ain't even gat time to blow you nose or scratch yuh balls. If you tek a break while machine working, cardboard pile up on you. Bai, we only glad when machine break down every other day so we get an extra half hour or hour break. And them thing heavy. All Writerji gat to do is move them crates and strap them cardboard tight. Is not easy work but he could control things at he own pace. Dhe man whistling and singing while he working as though nuthing bother he. Lunch time he finding time to talk with them Vietnamese girls. Since I working in dhat factory them Vietnamese don't mix with nobody. At break time at nine they sit in a group one side in the factory, lunch time they sit there, and afternoon break they sit there. Them two Vietnamese men watching Writerji carefully but soon he gat them girls laughing, and they saying hello now when they passing, and he know all they name. Writerji dressing smart and comb he hair everytime he go to the toilet, soon he in the office talking to dhe payroll clerk, Annette, who uncle own dhe factory. She really pretty and she rarely come into the factory until Writerji start talking with she now and again during lunch time. The office mek with plex-iglass and them office people could see everything happening in the factory. Soon she lending Writerji book. He just smiling when I ask he and saying is just literature. He trying to catch up on Canadian Literature.

Don't let mih tell yuh, dhem white man in the factory vex. They gat all them forklift and checker and loader and super-visor and manager jobs but Annette ain't bothering with dhem. Lunch time and break time them big-bais alone in the lunch room. Only Ravi with them. Ravi come from Sri Lanka and he is senior floor hand – them supervisor give he order and he give we order. And he feel superior. He working there long and feel he is white man too. He don't mix with we. All them floor hands Guyanese or Trini Indians, Sri Lankans or Vietnamese – and it look like everybody refugee. Soon the foreman start finding extra work for Writerji. As soon as Writerji finish strapping, he gat to come and help we on line, help with the forklift, clean up the factory floor, help with checking, help with dhis and dhat. Writerji still smiling but he hardly talking to Annette except when he gat to go and collect he paycheque from she every Friday afternoon. She and he talking on phone night time, and weekend she coming for Writerji and they going for lunch or din-ner. Writerji ain't going no place except work if he ain't get car. April coming and every morning at dhe bus stop Writerji grum-bling about dhe blasted Canadian cold – and how dhe blasted foreman picking on he.

This lunch time Writerji just done eating and he can't bear it. He walk straight in dhe office and give Annette a book, and spend two minutes chatting with she. And everybody could see what happening with dhem. Is love like first time. As soon as he come out dhe office and sit down next to me, the foreman come out the lunch room.

"Anand – this lunch room need cleaning and sweeping. Go and give it a clean out."

"I'm on lunchbreak now Tony." Writerji sounding sharp and everybody listening. The factory silent, nat a machine working. You know how in a factory everything close down because everybody get break same time.

"Well, things slack now. . . ."

Writerji cut him off and speaking louder. "Listen, Tony, I said I'm on my lunch break. Talk to me after my break. Do you understand simple English?"

"You Paki teaching me about English?"

"I'm not a Paki. See, you don't even know geography!"

"All right, smart ass. Clean and sweep this lunch room after break – here's the broom."

Writerji jump up and I get up too. I thinking he gun knock the foreman. "Let me tell you something, Tony. You can take that broom and shove it. I don't eat in that lunch room. Let the pigs who eat in there clean it up."

"You're fired, man. You're fired."

Writerji laugh loud and touch he waist. "O course I'm fired! Jealous son-of-a-bitch! And you think I'm scared, yeh! I had enough, yeh. I quit anyway, yeh!" He imitating the Canadian accent perfect perfect. I want laugh, but I thinking about meself so I hold in till Tony rush to the office. Writerji pick up he things and walk to dhe office, everybody watching as he bend down and whisper something in Annette ear and kiss she cheek. And she get up and follow he to dhe door. Night time Writerji tell me and Hermit he thinking about heading for New York. Same time Hermit lawyer just file my papers and he seh things look good fuh mih so I holding on. Writerji seh he ain't able with this cold and stupid Canadians, and he jus call he cousin in New York. New York warmer and things easier. The biggest joke is that he cousin give he two names in Toronto to contact in the "backtrack" ring to smuggle he across dhe border and one a dhe people is Hermit self!

Well, next day late winter storm – one foot snow and cold cold. Minus fifteen degrees and with wind chill like minus thirty. Confusion on dhem road. People hardly go to wuk. I stay home. Writerji said he cut right card. He going to New York, he ain't staying for next Canadian winter. Two days later, is Friday, and everything running. Temperature warm up to minus two and road salted and clear, sunshine. Friday afternoon after work Annette come and she and Writerji gone out. Dhe man feel free like a bird. He stap grumbling about Canadian cold now he decide to head south. Half past five and place dark already. Me and Hermit done eat and looking news when, bam bam bam on dhe door. We think Writerji come back, forget he key or something. Is good thing is Hermit open dhe door. Two immigration officer get tip that an illegal alien name Anand living here. Man I nearly get heart attack. Hermit checking dhem ID and talking to them officer like is he own buddy and he invite them officer in for coffee – cold night for this work, he telling them. Hermit say is just the two a-we live there. He show dhem ID and tell them how lawyer file paper fuh me. I not working, he say, just waiting for my case, and he send me for mih passport and immigration papers. I sweating and praying dhat Writerji don't turn up then. After he tell dhem I ain't working I feeling better. I afraid I might say something wrang.

Finally them officer gone – apologize to we, man them men nice and pleasant and apologize. Hermit seh when dhem gane, don't let them smile fool yuh. Well, is time to move Writerji. When Writerji come home is late. We looking TV and waiting fuh he but is he and Annette come in quiet quiet. Writerji laugh when he see we up. Well, we gat to wait till next morning. We done know why dhem come in so quiet quiet like fowl thief. We mek excuse and hustle to bed closing we room door and left them on dhe settee.

Next morning Writerji blue when we give he dhe lowdown. He seh he certain is Tony. Yuh think Writerji would lie low after this! Dhat bai now get bad to go out. And Annette teking day off from work. . . .

Yuh think is lil story we go through nuh. When Writerji ready fuh leave, is how you think he cross the border. Well, a gun tell you, but still secret. Yuh think Writerji can write dhis? Is in a container truck. Special container, forty-foot container. Them bai moving genuine shipment of furniture and personal effects to the States. Yuh know people always moving back and forth to States legally. A separate section in dhe front of dhe container conceal real good – double wall – to hold four people. That is how. Can't give more details as dhem bai still using dhe route. And Hermit seh less I know, less I talk. Well he didn't figure on Writerji. Writerji disappear underground in New York and is years we hear nothing about he. Next thing we know is novel out set in Guyana, and then dhem "Underground Stories" by a writer name S T Writerji! He mixing up place and incident between New York and Canada – who can tell what is what? But them thing real and only we know who is who. Writerji send Hermit book to mih house. When Hermit, Lena, and them children come over Hermit quiet quiet. Is summer and we barbecuing in the back yard and dhem children running around, just like now. He find a corner and read that book right out. Nat a man disturb he. Lena surprise but nat me, dhat is dhe Hermit I know. When he done he shake he head and come over and tek a drink. Ask Lena and Katie. We drinking in mih house. Tears run down he eyes. No, that bai nat like Naipaul, he seh. He mek we proud! Dhem days, dhem days right hey, mixup and sanaay, sanaay good like rice and daal, and nice hot seven curry with hot chatney. I read dhat book out, right out dhe night before, and was same way I feel. Hermit tek a next drink – I gat a special bottle 12 Year Old Demerara Gold – and he come and sit next to me. Ask he when yuh see he. And he point to dhe front page. Writerji mek dedication –

To Hermit and Jones

– and he seh, "dhem days, bai, dhem days is something else. See what we gain from dhem!" He close dhe book – just so and tears run down he face. Ask he, ask Hermit when yuh see him, ask him about dhat, about Writerji, about we.

TERENCE YOUNG

The Berlin Wall

Marilyn tells the boy right on the hall stairs that these are her children's rooms she is renting out. The yellow is Karen's and the blue is Daniel's. She doesn't tell him both children would probably be in their rooms this very minute playing video games or reading comics if her husband hadn't been such a stupid man and she had not been an even stupider woman.

"I must share this room?" the boy asks.

Marilyn's eyes are level with his, but the prospective boarder stands two steps below her. His backpack is decorated with baggage tags and a hand-stitched German flag.

"My children aren't here right now," she says.

"It is still their rooms, of course. I understand this." The boy blinks twice and pushes his glasses higher up the bridge of his nose.

"You can use this one for as long as you want," Marilyn says.

"Perhaps your children will want their rooms back one day?" the boy asks.

Marilyn turns and heads up to the second-floor landing. "Not if they have any brains," she says.

She opens the door to her daughter's room and steps aside to let the young German enter. The hinges protest slightly, and although she has been renting out these rooms for almost five months, she still experiences the brief hope that Karen will be waiting on the other side. The room is pretty bare bones, but clean. The walls have been relieved of posters and only a couple of specimens from her daughter's collection of perfume bottles remain on the bureau. It is a bedroom, after all. The boy takes off his pack and sits it upright on the bed. He is what she expected a German to look like. She finds it disappointing just to be in the same room with him. His hair is a dusty haystack. And the glasses are round ones with thin wire frames. His passport says he is seventeen.

"I like this room very much," he says.

Out in the garden, Mac is on his knees planting some thinnings a neighbour has given him: a dozen Swiss chard plants and six kale. The pale fronds of Swiss chard lie limp and unenthusiastic on the dark soil while Mac attends to the kale. Marilyn doesn't like greens of any kind. Neither does Mac. Most vegetables, for that matter. He gives the bulk of what he grows to friends or serves it to the boarders. Once in a while he makes Marilyn drive him down to the food bank, where he leaves a sack of whatever is in season. Just now it is tomatoes and corn and beets. Above him, a window swings open, and Mac sees a blond head peer out over the ragtag back yards of the neighbourhood. The head scans the rooftops in a slow semicircle, stopping midway to take in the sea glimpse, and then lowers its gaze to the garden. When it sees Mac, an arm joins the head and waves. Mac raises his trowel in a kind of salute.

"Okay," the head says. "All right, man."

Mac moved in with his niece Marilyn after his wife died exactly a year ago this September the fifth, not long after Marilyn lost the kids. Mac is a retired small engine mechanic. Weedeaters, leaf blowers, roto-tillers. Just before he stopped working, he had learned everything there was to know about the snowmobile. His wife died in Paris, in a room on the top floor of the Hotel Garnier, near the train station. He brought her ashes home in a carry-on and scattered them in the bay not too far from Marilyn's house. Up until Emily's death, she and Mac spent two weeks of every summer camped in the driveway of Marilyn and Evan's faded clapboard two-storey in Newport,

Oregon. It was as close to the sea as they could afford and, until the trip to France, the farthest they'd ever travelled outside their home in Whitefish, Montana.

Mac rented a boat for Emily's burial at sea. On the way back to the marina, the motor cut out, and Mac had to take the cover off the outboard to adjust the mixture. When he told the rental people what he'd done, they offered him a job filling in on weekends. He pays Marilyn two hundred a month to sleep in the den, the room at the front of the house Marilyn's husband Evan used to call his office. Evan sold dope. Mollycoddled, fertilizer-fed, house-bound marijuana raised under thirty grow-lamps that cost a fortune in electricity every month. When the power authority decided to share the consumption rates of its customers with the state police, Evan went to jail. A drug squad stripped the attic of ninety healthy plants, an acre of tin foil, three boxes of spent bulbs, and fifteen gallons of liquid nutrient. After they left, child apprehension services made a case for Karen and Daniel – phoned by a neighbour? the school? – and within a week they were gone, too. Marilyn got to keep the house.

"We should take in boarders," Mac suggested to Marilyn after six months. She had snagged work cleaning offices after hours, but it clearly wasn't enough. Her two-year college diploma in criminology was next to useless, though she was now qualified to work as a prison guard, an irony which she was not yet prepared to acknowledge. Mac told her, "My cooking skills need some stretching and you could use the money."

The people they let out the rooms to are usually tourists who come to spend a few days, sometimes as long as two weeks, in this quiet town next to the ocean. Mac prepares the meals, keeps the bathrooms tolerable, washes up. Marilyn pins notices to telephone poles, takes calls. Summer fare is steady in Newport, word gets around. At night, from his hide-a-bed in the den, Mac can hear the low murmur of couples as they review their day, plan the next. He hears doors open in the middle of the night as men and women haul themselves out of their dreams for a trip to the bathroom. He hears their lovemaking, too, a sound he always likes because it puts him into the deepest of sleeps.

Sometimes the boarders leave things. Rocks they pick up on their strolls by the bay, brochures from the harbour hotels. And other things. Once, while he was cleaning under the bed in Karen's old room, he found a straight razor, the blade worn into a curve and the ivory handle yellow with age. The discovery puzzled him because the person who had just vacated the room was a woman. He put the razor into a box in the basement along with everything else he'd found. He usually tries to track down the owner if he thinks the article might be missed, but he's had no luck with the razor.

Marilyn sits in the kitchen reading over the letter from the local branch of the Rotary Club. It came yesterday:

Dear Fo'c'sle Boarding House,

The Newport Branch of the Harbourside Rotarians wishes to thank you for acting as host family for this year's exchange student, Dieter Lippa. We hope you will attend the formal welcome dinner taking place Saturday, September 21st, at 7:00 p.m. in the Travelodge.

Sincerely,
Peter Trippet
Treasurer: Harbourside Rotarians, District 502

Mac tells Marilyn the student is a gift-horse. Winter trade, he says, that's what they need. The Rotary people are a steady paycheque. Let them throw a little money her way. Mac makes everything sound exciting. She places the correspondence into a cake tin. From the same tin she pulls out the postcards she received from her children during their summer vacation. They went to Disneyland for two weeks with Marilyn's mother and father, into whose hands the state had seen fit to place Karen and Daniel. Marilyn would have preferred total strangers. Her parents perform their foster duties as though they are administering a regimen of therapeutic drugs. Visits occur only when they permit them and always at their home. Marilyn manages to bite her tongue most of the time.

The kids' postcards didn't arrive at Marilyn's house until after the trip was over. Karen phoned to ask if she had received them.

"No," Marilyn told her, "not yet." Daniel giggled on the extension. Marilyn pictured Karen in the kitchen of her parents' home in Eugene, and Daniel in the living-room, but, really, she had no idea where they were at all. The two of them yelled through the earpiece at her in disbelief.

"Of course you have them, silly," Daniel said. "We mailed them to you." Marilyn could think of nothing to say in return. Was this a test? Then her mother came on from somewhere else.

"How's my baby brother," she asked, yelling, too. "Marilyn, how's Mac?"

Marilyn saw herself holding three very long black strings, each with a gaping mouth at the end. She didn't want to listen. To hear her children talk about themselves as though they were distant relatives, to digest the chunks her mother had bitten out of their days to pass on like gossip. She wanted to hang up, to cut the connection without even wishing them good-bye. She lied instead, told them someone was at the door. A strategical error, she thought as she placed the receiver in its cradle. There'd be little chance now of them coming home for the start of the school year. When the vacation mail came the next day, she phoned to tell them, but her mother said they were outside playing.

She riffles the correspondence as though it were a deck of cards. There's the one of the Conestoga Hotel. Karen wrote out the menu for room service and underlined her favourites. *We went swimming in the rain*, she wrote at the very bottom. Another one shows the Pirates of the Caribbean with a circle inked in on the photo. *We stood here* in tiny letters fills the circle. From an envelope, Marilyn pulls out two framed silhouettes, one of Karen and another of Daniel. The letter that came with the silhouettes describes how the man who made them used nothing more than a pair of scissors and his two eyes. She recognizes the black outlines of her children, can distinguish each one easily. There are a few letters from Evan mixed in with the children's mail but she feels no urge to give them a second read. His high-school scrawl hasn't changed. She sees where he has written PWB at the bottom of an envelope. Please Write Back. As though he's been caught skipping class and this is another note smuggled out of the detention hall. She returns the thin stack of cards and letters to the tin and closes the lid, disgusted with herself.

Marilyn looks out the window at Mac working in the garden. Before he came to stay – in the two months after Evan was jailed and Karen and Daniel had gone to live with their grandparents – she used to walk out in the evenings to the floating fish and chip sit-in/take-out next to the boat rental at the marina. Cooking for one was an art that eluded her. She would sit in one of the white plastic chairs littered about the wharf and listen to the boats nudge up against their moorings, feel the decking rise and fall with the wake of passing boats. Even when both rooms are taken and Mac has dinner on the table, she will occasionally stroll down. Taking the night off, Mac calls it. She watches him press his fingers into the soil around the base of some green thing he is planting. He is a man, as she gratefully knows, who will take her to her grave if he has to.

Dieter Lippa wakes to his third morning in America. He showers and brushes his teeth and pees a bright red stream of pee. The beets, he decides. He comes downstairs and drinks a cup of coffee with the old man, who tells Dieter to call him Mac. Dieter then walks two blocks to Seaview High School.

"Hello," he says to a bowl-headed boy in long baggy shorts. The boy balances a skateboard in one hand as though he were carrying a plank.

"My name is Dieter. I am from Germany." A girl and two other boys in shorts, also with skateboards, join Dieter and the bowl-headed boy.

"West or East?" the girl asks. She is wearing a full-length Indian skirt, a peasant blouse, and steel-toed boots.

"We are unified now," Dieter says. "One country, just like you."

"Cool," the girl says.

"Yes, it is," Dieter says. "It is very cool."

The girl's name is Bree and her brother is the bowl-headed boy. His name is Chris. They live in a house built by an inventor. It has eight sides and rotates.

"When I want the sun in my room, I just flick a switch," Bree says. She snaps her fingers to imitate the sound of a switch being flicked.

"What do you do if you both want the sun?" Dieter asks.

The morning scoots by. Dieter is given a timetable and a combination lock. He will be studying modern history, English, journalism, mathematics, and law. Dieter's homeroom teacher introduces him as the school's guest and a full member of this year's graduating class. She tells the thirty grade twelve students that this year could be one of the best in their lives, but that it will also be the last year they will all be together like this. Then she lets them go. Dieter walks with Bree and Chris down to the bay. Chris wants to meet some friends at the skateboard park. When they arrive, there are a few boys clinging to the edge of a smooth cement crater. The boys release themselves one at a time and skate down the curving sides of the bowl to the centre, where there is a large round hump. They climb the hump until they can climb no farther and then they flip and turn in mid-air to skate back down. Dieter and Bree watch Chris launch himself into the bowl.

"Did you ever get to see it?" Bree asks. They are lying on the grass bank that leads down to the beach. The smell of oil mixed with gas rises on the wind from the marina at the far end of the bay.

"All my life they tell me there is the wall," Dieter says, "and then last year it comes down when I have been only one time ever to Berlin as a child."

"But it was big, wasn't it?" Bree asks. "It was a real wall, not just some yellow line painted on the ground."

"It was a real wall," Dieter says.

"You are so lucky," Bree says.

Bree and Chris walk past Dieter's house on the way home. He points it out and tells them his room is on the second floor. Chris tells him he's crazy. Dieter asks him why, but Chris doesn't answer. He just purses his lips together and inhales deeply, holding the air in his lungs for a long time and crossing his eyes.

Saturday morning, Mac takes the early shift at the boat rental. Three fishermen show up wanting one of the fourteen-footers. Mac places their deposit in the till and loads them up with life jackets and a tank of gas. He checks for licences. The men are carrying thermoses and blankets for the fog. Their rods are old, the guides rusty.

"We'll be lucky if we catch bottom," one of the men jokes to another.

"Enough of that," Mac says.

The day is muted. Sunlight, the fall air, the engine's watery exhaust. Mac can tell these are not seasoned sportsmen. They might as well be boarding a train, or buying tickets to a movie. The three step gingerly into the boat alongside all their gear and within five minutes disappear around the point. Mac can't help wondering if he'll see them again.

Mac's first attempt to fly home with his wife was a failure. Going through customs he was stopped by an official who wanted to see the contents of the cardboard box containing Emily's ashes. The weight of the box disturbed the official, even though it did not register as metal on the scanner. When he discovered the true nature of what the box contained, he refused Mac permission to board his flight.

"The transportation of human remains," he said, "is a serious matter."

The funeral parlour had said nothing about airline policy; neither had the police. Mac returned to the same hotel he had just booked out of and was given the same room he had just vacated. He asked for a single but none was available. He spent another five days in Paris, two longer than he and Emily had originally planned. He walked through the Bois de Boulogne again. He revisited La Rue Mouffetard and got drunk at La Negre Joyeuse. He bought chestnuts from the man outside Notre Dame. By the time the documentation arrived permitting him to return home, he had begun to wonder what his hurry was.

The three fishermen return by eleven o'clock. They have caught two mudsharks that lie belly-up in their own blood on the flat bottom of the aluminum boat. None of the three wants the fish, and after they leave Mac slips them over the side where they sink slowly into the darkness under the pilings. In the afternoon he stops at a bar on the way home, a nautical place with oak decking on the ceiling and a wall of windows overlooking the bay. Mac likes to invent cocktail combinations to confuse the bartenders. Today he orders a Peach and Frog. He tells the waiter it's a Harvey Wallbanger with creme de menthe instead of grenadine. Last week he ordered a Chinchilla: an ounce of Cinzano in a pint of Guinness. Tomorrow, he and Marilyn will drive the eighty miles to Eugene where his sister lives so that Marilyn can visit her children.

Marilyn comes in around seven o'clock dripping wet.

She went out for fish and chips and the chair she was sitting in collapsed, tipping her over the edge of the wharf. The young cook lifted her out. He threw himself flat, reached under her arms, and pulled her up. She lost her change purse and a pair of sunglasses. The cook said they'd send a diver down for them in the morning. People applauded and someone brought a blanket for Marilyn. She thanked the man but her heart was not in it. The water had been so dark and warm, an unexpected blessing, far too brief.

Now she sits across from Dieter's new friend Bree at the kitchen table, the blanket still around her shoulders. She holds a cup of coffee between her two hands, circling it with her fingers, the handle facing away.

"So if all you get is minimum wage," Bree is saying, "how do you live?" Backpacks heavy with schoolbooks lie against the back door like fallen fruit.

"I rent rooms." Marilyn nods her head upward in the direction of Dieter's room.

Bree bends her head down to the table, sips her own coffee without raising the cup. "Dieter says they're your kids' rooms."

"They are," Marilyn says.

"And that man that made dinner tonight, the old guy. I sometimes see him at the marina. Dieter says he lives here."

"He does," Marilyn says.

"Is he like your father or something?" Bree asks.

"My uncle," Marilyn says.

Dieter returns from the bathroom and sits down. Marilyn knows he and Bree are being solicitous because of her mishap, but she has no wish to talk to either of them. Mac is in the den reading.

"Your house got busted, right?" Bree asks.

"About a year ago," Marilyn says. Dieter is smiling across at her. He holds a cigarette aloft in one hand as though he is posing for a magazine.

"And that's why your children don't live with you any more, right?" Bree takes the cigarette from Dieter and puts it out.

"They're with my parents until my probation ends. Maybe sooner," Marilyn says.

"Harsh," Bree says.

Nobody believes Marilyn could have lived in the same house with Evan and not known what he was up to. Marilyn's parents have expressed the opinion that probably she should have gone to jail, too. She thought Evan was building an addition. This is what he did for a living. Sundecks, garages, basement suites. Why shouldn't he do it at home? There was plumbing, there was wiring, there was wood and nails. It was a lot like their marriage. There were children, a house, the ten years they'd spent together, every outward sign that something solid was forming, something durable. That's why she feels uncomfortable around these kids. Their trust is a little too familiar. To his credit, Evan did his best not to implicate Marilyn. She was given two years' probation. If Child Services hadn't been alerted to her case, Marilyn might have considered herself lucky.

"I should get to bed," Marilyn says. She rises and heads down the hallway to her room.

"Have a bath," Bree says.

The next day, Marilyn is too sick to stand. She debates having Mac and Dieter carry her to the car so that she can make the two-hour trip to see Karen and Daniel. It is never a good idea to cancel a scheduled visit, but in the end she phones to say she cannot come.

The night of the Rotary dinner, Dieter, Bree, Marilyn, and Mac climb into the still immaculate interior of Evan's '72 Cutlass Supreme and drive two miles to the Newport Travelodge, recently renovated to offer full convention facilities. The sun is still up when they arrive, perched above the Pacific, ready to drop. It is the last day of summer, the equinox. Patches of evening fog swirl past, blown inland by the onshore breeze, pale dervishes who wrap themselves around poles, the aerials of parked cars. Dieter is giving a speech tonight and everyone has dressed for the occasion. Mac pressed his grey flannels and polished his Rockports. Marilyn traded her jeans for a white wraparound skirt. Bree is wearing a full-length black sleeveless dress which stops just above her boots. Her hair has grown slightly from the close shave she treated herself to at the beginning of school. Mac lent Dieter a sports jacket to go with his white shirt and corduroys.

They troop through a small lobby and stop at the request of a man sitting behind a table whose job it is to provide everyone with a name tag. He writes in bold block letters with a black felt pen and peels back a Teflon strip so that each person can stick his tag in a prominent place. Bree places hers immediately on her forehead. They walk into the Buccaneer Room. Heavy rope nets hang from the ceiling, hiding duct work and plumbing. The walls have been painted into one long tropical scene of palm-covered islands and sailing ships flying skull-and-crossbones flags. The prow of a wooden lifeboat protrudes halfway into the room. It's the buffet. The pirate theme depresses Marilyn until she remembers Karen's postcard, and then she perks right up. Bree weaves through the room to a table near the podium and the others follow.

"We won't miss a word here," she says.

Each table seats eight. Two carafes of wine – one red, one white – stand in the middle of each of the thirty round tablecloths. A few people are seated already, their glasses full, but many more are in a line leading to the bar. Mac crosses the carpet to join it. A couple of men in suits approach Marilyn and Dieter.

"Hey," one man says.

"You made it," says the other. He looks at Dieter's name tag. "Dieter, isn't it," he asks, rhyming Dieter with "lighter."

"Yes, but . . ." Dieter says.

"I'm Peter. This is John Prentice." There is a flurry of handshaking.

"Look," John says. "You've really drawn a crowd tonight. People are coming out of the woodwork for this. Can I get you something, Mrs. . . . ?" He looks in vain at her chest.

"Morgan," Marilyn says.

"Can I get you something to drink, Mrs. Morgan?" he asks.

"Sure," Marilyn says. "That'd be nice. How about a Chinchilla?"

"Sounds good," John says. He turns to Bree. "How about you, Miss? Dieter? Coke okay?"

Peter Trippet explains the schedule of events to them: introductions, dinner, the treasurer's report, three short talks by members of the student club of public speaking, and finally their star attraction, Dieter, who will be speaking on the effects of unification.

"So, enjoy," he says before working his way to the podium.

John returns a few minutes later with Marilyn's drink and two cokes for Dieter and Bree.

"The bartender was stumped," he tells Marilyn, "until this gentleman filled him in." Mac sits down with a drink of his own.

"What do you have there?" Marilyn asks him.

"A Thumbelina," Mac says.

Table numbers are drawn out of a hat to see who goes to the buffet first. Beside Marilyn sit the president of the local branch of the Bank of America and his wife. Another man who introduces himself as an accountant for Weyerhaeuser also joins the table. The chair to Bree's right remains empty. The bank president has been told that Marilyn runs the boarding house where

the guest speaker is staying, and he tells her he is pleased to see
the spirit of free enterprise alive and well in Newport.

"Alive, anyway," Marilyn says. She feels his eyes staring at
her hand, the sudden weight of her wedding ring.

"What about your husband?" he asks. "What does he do?"

"He's dead," she says.

Their table number is called. They pick up plates and walk
past bean salads and cold cuts, crab legs and lasagne, roast potatoes, lamb curry, and a chef slicing off slabs of beef. Everyone
takes a little of everything except Bree, whose plate bears only
caesar salad, two potatoes, and bread. They return to find the
waiters have replaced empty carafes with full ones.

"It's on railway tracks," Bree is saying to the accountant as
she sits down. "Every room moves but the bathroom."

"I see," the accountant says.

When the police came through the front and back doors of the
house on that muggy July Saturday, Marilyn was at the King
Koin laundromat sorting through a basket of work socks, divid-
ing them into keepers, menders, and hopeless. Earlier she had
dropped Karen and Daniel off for the day at a friend's. She'd left
Evan up in the attic hammering away at something, so very
probably he didn't hear them knocking, if they knocked at all.
Marilyn likes to believe there was a certain amount of civility
to the event – she avoids the word *raid* – perhaps a polite tap at
the window first, a shout through the screen door off the back
deck. She doesn't see any guns or dogs or truncheons in her ver-
sion of things, and while she is familiar with the pale gear of the
Oregon State Police, she prefers to think of the intruders wearing faded jeans and work-shirts. When she arrived home from
doing the laundry, she found a small crowd of people gathered
outside her house. A few neighbours recognized her and waved
as she pulled up. As Marilyn ran from the car to the house,
her first thought was that Evan had started a house fire. She
expected to see smoke billowing out from under the eaves, and
she experienced a brief moment of relief when she remembered
where the children were. The likelihood of a fire – Evan with a
plumbing torch, his inadvertently igniting one of the beams?

rafters? – stayed with her as she stepped over the front door
wrenched from its hinges. Once inside, she saw furniture
turned over, pictures pulled from the walls, plants torn out by
the roots and soil emptied from pots onto the carpets. The fire
in her mind was becoming a crazy fire, a fire that eluded capture, one that had to be chased though all the rooms of the
house. Evan was nowhere. It wasn't until she went out into the
back yard and asked an officer taking notes what had happened
that she found out the truth. He gave her a card and a number
to call, and when she asked him if she was going to be arrested,
too, he said not today.

The third of the three public speakers is a teenage girl in a wheelchair. She speaks about her life before the accident, the teams
she played on. She describes a typical Friday night with her
friends, and how a single error in judgment changed everything.
At the end of her speech she repeats the word *forever*, allowing
a pause of several seconds between each *forever*. Dieter begins
clapping immediately and so enthusiastically the whole room
soon joins in. Some of the people seem not to know what they
are clapping for, steeped as they are by now in several carafes of
wine, but they clap anyway. Two men lift the girl, wheelchair
and all, from the raised platform which serves as a stage, and
Peter Trippet readjusts the microphone. Then it is Dieter's turn.
    People are stirring cups of coffee and several conversations
have grown in volume to arguments when Dieter starts to
address the crowd.
    "It is for me a great joy tonight to speak to you about my
country," he says over the rising din. Behind Marilyn, a deep
voice rumbles something derisively unintelligible.
    "Since I am young," Dieter continues, "there are stories
told in my family about people who once were our friends and
neighbours."
    "Louder!" someone in the back yells.
    Dieter waves at the person and leans closer to the micro-
phone. "These people disappeared when Germany was cut into
two."
    "Good riddance," the man with the deep voice baritones.

"Nobody has seen them for forty years," Dieter says. "This is an awful thing for your friends to be somewhere else."

Marilyn finds she cannot concentrate on Dieter's words. She squints to block out everything except Dieter's face. She cups her hands around her ears, but it does no good. Snatches of his speech drift in and out of focus like snowflakes passing through a beam of light.

"The wall was everywhere," she hears him say, "not just Berlin."

"Missiles in the streets of my town," he says.

She glances at Mac sitting next to her. He is taking small sips from his cup of coffee. To Mac's right, she sees Bree with her dress hiked up and her legs crossed in a half Lotus. She rests one boot assertively on top of her right knee. Her hands are clasped behind her neck and she is chewing a piece of gum. Tomorrow is autumn, Marilyn remembers. We are passing from one season to another at this very moment. She pictures the equinox like some ghostly curtain suspended in space, and the earth moving through it to the other side. Special sight, she once believed, was what allowed her to detect the rotation of the earth through her bedroom window, but a friend pointed out it was only the clouds passing that gave her the impression of movement. Marilyn closes her eyes, shutting out Dieter, the drunken Rotarians. She leans back heavily, sinking into the armrests, imagines a wind blowing the hair from her face, the fall giving way invisibly before her.

Although the picture the next day shows Dieter with his face in Marilyn's lap, her hands supporting it, a better angle would reveal that most of his body is lying on the table, and that only a little bit of him – his head and neck, possibly one of his shoulders – is guilty of any impropriety. An even wider view would capture Bree with her left leg fully extended and the tip of one steel-toed boot about to make contact with the stomach of the rude and heavily intoxicated war veteran, who, in a fit of pique, staggers to the podium and drags Dieter from his perch and hurls him across the special guest's table, past the accountant, the bank president, and his wife, almost into the arms or lap of Marilyn, who has woken from a soothing reverie about time and space to see Mac doing his best to pin the rude man's arms behind his back and Peter Trippet yanking at Bree's dress.

"Fascist!" Bree is screaming at the man. "You stupid fuck!"

For his part, the veteran is yelling even more loudly. "Dumb-ass kraut," he spits out at Dieter, who is still trying to extricate himself from tablecloth, glasses, cutlery. "I'll show you missiles," he says. "I'll show you fucking bombs."

The crowd is thinning. People are picking up hats and purses, donning jackets, preparing to slip out the double-doored exit at the side of the room. Marilyn looks down at Dieter struggling to right himself. As young as he is, she thinks, there is something old about this boy, the folds of skin that crease the back of his neck, perhaps – something very European, certainly – and she lifts his head gently like a bowl, right into line with the lens of the camera.

BRIAN BARTLETT

Thomas, Naked

Were heavy wings beating by his ears? Was some great engine roaring, gears cracking in the dark? As he slowly woke up, squirming on his stiff back, the old man felt the house tilt. Why was his bed sliding across the floor? Why had his family left the window open, snakes of cold air sliding around his neck, under the blankets?

With his eyes finally open, he saw speckled blackness whirling overhead, stars maybe making those sounds. House? He wasn't in any house. He turned his head to one side: semi-lit office buildings silhouetted, smudged distant streetlights, camel-backed snowbanks – then, closer by, skaters rushing past all around him, skates cutting and chipping the ice. Young and old strangers shuffled, lunged, floated along the frozen canal. His leg itched inside its cast.

The toboggan slowed down, wobbled, stopped.

He'd never slept a wink in cars or on buses and planes, so he was frightened that he'd done so on a loose-slatted toboggan, despite the racket of it striking bumpy ice under him and a wild vibration shaking his backbone. Was his body failing him so much that it had learned to fall asleep even in such places? He wouldn't let his granddaughter know.

She bent towards him, moonlit glass earrings bouncing below her ski-hat. "Still alive?" she asked. The toboggan darted ahead a few feet, then just as abruptly stopped again, but he was pointed backwards, the wrong way to see her husband holding the rope.

"Barely," he said, reaching under the blankets for his hand-kerchief.

"Need any help?"

Just because I broke my leg, he wanted to say, *doesn't mean I can't blow my nose.*

Carmen cupped her hands at the sides of her mouth and shouted at Percy to get moving again. The toboggan lurched so suddenly that the blankets went askew and the end of the cast slid outside them, rising like a mound of greying snow. On its way again, the toboggan banged against bumps the size of hail-stones, sounded like a set of boards and nails about to fly apart. When would they stop and open the thermos of hot black coffee, so he could breathe in the smell he craved? The blankets kept creeping up or slipping to one side. He felt like a patient in an absurd unravelling straitjacket.

He, Thomas Smart (Senior Maritime Speedskating Champion, 1935 to '37), could've skated rings around anyone in sight, if only his leg weren't broken. Instead, ignominiously, he was being dragged up and down the canal. *Ignominiously* – a word he'd hardly realized he knew, but so apt he might've waited all his life for it to fit this winter. He wanted to black out all memories of New Year's Eve, when he'd tripped on a beer can ice-locked into the canal, then twisted on his back and kicked the air with his skates, his bladder emptied by the shocks of pain flashing stronger and stronger through his leg, the stars overhead jumping like bits of shattered glass. He'd heard himself whim-pering like a dog.

From the toboggan, he could see two cross-country skiers beside the canal, slipping along a trail with matching unchang-ing rhythms. Closer by, an Irish setter trotted past on the ice, doing well, nothing like a comic-strip dog scrambling with its legs all one blur. Saliva sparkled on its tongue; its panted breath shaped clouds in the cold air.

Over the canal, stars were like optical illusions or dirt specks on his glasses. He pulled off his glasses, breathed on them, clum-sily rubbed them on the top blanket. When he looked again, the stars still seemed fuzzy and bloated. Did he need to see an eye-doctor? In the past year, he'd sensed Amelia's absence – and presence – under a night sky more than anywhere else. After she had died a few minutes before midnight, the sky outside the hospital felt like a truckload of logs on his shoulders while he walked numbly to the car, sliding over unsanded parking-lot ice, still feeling her feverish hand in his.

Often when he woke up in the morning now he thought of questions he'd never asked her in their forty-six years together:

When I hear you crack your knuckles, why do I hate it?

What makes you tape pictures from National Geographic *to the fridge?*

Would you want to visit the North Pole or the equator?

Do you believe in anything like angels?

Once he'd been a talkative man – but never a good listener, she'd always said. With Julie and her family, he now often found himself giving quick, brief answers, as if all the changes – selling Smart's Kennels, renting his house, moving from Fredericton to Ottawa – had tied his tongue.

Still alive?

Barely.

Her legs pumping harder, Carmen slipped out of his sight, maybe to join Percy at the end of the rope. Thomas lifted his head and looked around again:

The scarred bulk of a closed fish-'n'-chips wagon. Shadowy skaters disappearing in the distance. A lone black skate abandoned, stranded on the ice.

In the summer, when Percy and Carmen had driven him to Montreal to see the Ramses II exhibit, he'd gazed at the statue of some moon-faced woman (a daughter of Ramses and Nefertari?) and – though her nose was broken off and a crown perched on her head – he'd thought, *That's Amelia so much I can hardly bear to look at it.*

Statues and pictures of proud imperial rulers made him imagine starving, mud-blinded, sun-blistered slaves in the Bible story, Jehovah's chosen collapsing in the heat. When he mumbled something about this, Carmen clucked her tongue and, for once sounding like her mother, said, *Aren't we morose today?* then turned to inspect a jewellery box. So much for the slaves –

and she a would-be social worker, he told himself, straightening his glasses to peer at the moon-faced Egyptian from a different angle. Again, the Egyptian looked like Amelia: that chin, that forehead, those eye-sockets. The rest of the afternoon he said little more; when they ate french fries on the steps outside, he wouldn't answer little Nat's and Sammy's questions, and he dipped his fries in ketchup so slowly he might've been hypnotized. On the way back to Ottawa, fanning himself with an exhibit brochure, exhausted by the heat and the distance travelled, he kept imagining those slaves as if *he* had barked out orders to have them whipped – as if like Ramses II he'd built a thousand-ton colossus of himself. Then he remembered the noseless, moon-faced woman again.

Why doesn't the heat make you bad-tempered, like it does me?

Would you want to go see the Pyramids?

Why do you love walking barefoot over beach rocks and sand?

Carmen was falling behind Percy again, even behind the toboggan where Thomas lay sluggish and motionless, at the mercy of others. She was skating stiffly with her arms straight at her sides. He lifted his head and was about to call out, *Use your whole body – your shoulders, your hips!* In six months or so she'd be in the hospital, to have a brother or sister for the twins. A sister, he hoped, his first great-granddaughter. A few years earlier, after the birth of the ninth grandson, he'd gone around joking, *Enough for my baseball team,* until he'd grown tired of his own quip.

More past moments sped through his head faster than the toboggan. Trapped, jolted and jarred, he felt as he did when a powerful headache and too many thoughts kept him awake while all he wanted was the oblivion of sleep. Why had he agreed to this idiocy, the night sky diving at him, the broken images of tilted and blurred skaters lurching in the distance?

Old-timers' baseball and hockey, jogging along the Green, refusing desserts – he'd been careful, so any lapses in his health seemed cruel and unjust, like fate slapping his face. For the past three days his bowels had been knotted; the gigantic bran muffins Percy baked had no effect. *Regular as clockwork*, he'd told a doctor in the fall, when he first suffered from constipation, *I've always been regular as clockwork*, then he pictured some clock lodged painfully inside his bowels.

Four generations in one house – far from common those days. Amelia had rarely spoken bluntly, but more than once she'd said, *The dogs mean more to you than we do*. Over the years Smart's Kennels had grown from ten cages to over a hundred. He was proud of it all – why not? But then he'd given it all up, as if there *were* wrong and shame attached to it. He'd never considered himself a sentimental sort, but in Ottawa he'd warmed to the idea of four generations living under one roof. He liked to think the arrangement honoured an earlier time, as if his family were surviving in some frontier, sticking together in the face of brutal elements and axe-wielding enemies.

Oh, but who was he fooling? For one thing, he knew it was an accident that Carmen had gotten pregnant in her and Percy's last year of college, so they'd married and turned Julie's basement into their home.

She had switched on her Walkman, distant jangling sounds mixing with sounds of skates scraping ice. She skated closer to him and shouted, "Want to hear some music?"

He twisted his face, as if to answer, *You want to torture me even more?*

Carmen smiled – with him more than at him, he felt sure – then she skated beyond him again. A few nights ago at the dinner table, he'd reached over to pat her stomach and slyly said (he hadn't joked much in the past year), *If this one's a boy, we'll leave it on someone's doorstep*, then Julie had made a sound with her lips and said, *What an awful thing to say, Dad. I should send you off to bed.*

Julie had always been like that – sombre, missing the point. So he couldn't fathom why she alone among his four kids hadn't said he was a fool to sell Smart's Kennels. Why she alone had invited him to move far from home and live under her roof. Why one night months after Amelia's death, the night he began sobbing helplessly as he'd never sobbed, she muted the TV and held him in her arms. After days of his weeping fits, she sent him to a Dr. Pack – a "grief counsellor" – for the first of several sessions, which he resented while they lasted but silently quoted from once they were finished. Yes, Julie had done what she could, but Carmen, Carmen with her green eyes and boyish haircut, smiled at him more than her mother ever had. Without her, without the twins crawling into his lap and Percy watching sports on TV with him, the house would've been like a dungeon and he like a king in exile among spiders and mould.

His ears and face ached with the cold. He wanted another pillow. He was bored by the black, star-filled sky. He hated the hailstone-sized bumps in the ice. He wanted Carmen to skate at his side and keep him company. He groped for his handkerchief. He felt there was a brick in his bowels. He wanted to scratch his knee. He needed a great-granddaughter. He hated Walkmans. He craved the coffee in Percy's knapsack. He wanted to be in bed, under half a dozen sheets and blankets, deep asleep. He imagined the canal thawing in an instant, the toboggan sinking with him to the bottom.

Orchestra music floated over the canal. The toboggan slowed down, wobbled, stopped.

Percy stood over him and asked in his mild, hushed way, "Tired yet?" Spears of frost jutted in strange, crooked shapes from his beard. All evening he and Carmen had been acting unusually attentive; this gave Thomas the distinct feeling that they were building up to breaking some news to him. He'd already guessed what the news was.

"Tired? Tired just lying here like a goddamn baby?"

"Thought you might be tired" was all Percy added, then he skated away. Thomas couldn't figure out a man who ate yogurt by the gallon and baked tofu casseroles, but during ball games on TV Percy had tried to cheer him up by quoting lines from the great manager Casey Stengel: *All right, fellas, line up alphabetically according to your height. . . . I never make predictions, especially about the future.*

An airplane flashed its lights high overhead. He wouldn't, he told himself, fall asleep again like some wretched convalescent clinging to his last threads of hope. He wouldn't be stubborn. He wouldn't mutter or bluster the next time Julie said, *Dad, all your ties are spotted with food*, or tugged the hair at the back of his neck and asked, *When did you last go to the barber?* or – leaving for her long hours as an MP's assistant – kissed him at the breakfast table, then wiped the lipstick off his cheek with a napkin. Patience had never been his greatest virtue, he'd told Dr. Pack. He wished it would toughen in him, like muscles hardening rather than going slack with age.

One of the crutches hidden under the blankets dug into his leg, and his back ached, vibrations hitting his spine like hammers. He lifted his head. Six little girls were holding hands but skating at different speeds, arranged like a twisted string of flowers. Three split to the left, three to the right, all their white skates looking brand new. In the space emptied by their disappearance, a tall stranger in black spandex, bent over almost parallel to the ice from the waist up, skated in smooth arcs as if along an obstacle course, graceful as a panther. Thomas saw himself skating in his heyday, felt Amelia's lips pressed against his the moment he stepped onto a walkway to a dressing-room with a trophy clutched in his hand (winner of the 220-yard, 880-yard, and one-mile events) – then dropped his head back onto the pillow, his neck worn out from the strain.

Why are Irish setters your favourite dogs?

How can you follow auctioneers when they babble on like that?

Did you forgive me for the time I grabbed your arm so hard my fingers left bruises?

Another abandoned skate – or was it the same one? Had they turned around without him even noticing?

The cast had crept back outside the blankets, moonlight shining on it. He strained his neck to stare at the ugly appendage, the humbling weight covered with signatures and good-luck messages: Julie's GET WELL, DAD, Percy's *HOPE YOURE HOPPING AGAIN SOON*, Carmen's **Model of the Year**.

Model of the Year. He'd answered an ad in the *Citizen* – "Wanted for one evening, male age 65-75, for nude modelling" – so

Julie would stop nagging him about his not getting out of the house enough, and he'd have something different to tell Dr. Pack. Besides, he was proud that he'd stayed lean as a speed-skater all his life. When he'd said, *An easy way to make a few bucks, just sitting there like the day I was born*, Julie gave him a scolding glance. Somehow he'd never expected the word "nude" really meant stark nakedness, so when he stripped to his bathing suit in the studio – a big barn-like room full of splotchy, violent, unfinished canvasses – and heard Ms. Krantz say, *Sorry, Mr. Smart, those trunks have to go too*, the joke was on him. Gazing at pipes and wires crisscrossing the ceiling, he plucked at his bathing suit; then – figuring that pulling his clothes back on and rushing away, undrawn and unpaid, would've been as shameful as anything – he granted Ms. Krantz and her dozen students their wish. The first few minutes, he couldn't think of much except mud-coloured skin blemishes, wrinkled thighs, steel-wool pubic hair, a thumb-like penis. He didn't dare look down at himself, but soon – amazingly soon – he felt as he had in dreams of walking naked down a street: perfectly relaxed, nothing in the world more natural. High winds hit the draughty windows, but Ms. Krantz had plugged in an electric heater close to him. Somehow he felt separated from his own body, as if he were sitting out there like everyone else, watching and drawing it.

Naked, he felt more stripped of himself than he ever had. He heard pencils rubbed against art paper, the words *bone . . . axis . . . corrugated . . . erase*. He didn't know what any of the words had to do with him, and he didn't care. He hadn't felt so utterly relaxed in a year. On the bus downtown an hour earlier he'd sat near some punks – filthy-mouthed punks in jean jackets or scraps of leather, jagged hair dangling down into their eyes – and after a while he'd wanted to kick them off the bus one by one, or slap them all senseless. How far away they – rather, his fury at them – now seemed. Naked, he felt he had the patience and calm to put up with anything.

In the warmth from the plugged-in heater, he thought of the blue veins above Amelia's breasts . . . of her halting walk in the years after she'd broken her knee-cap (never one to complain about her own pain) . . . of a glass bottle she'd inherited from her father. That bottle had a tiny model ship inside, along with a tiny sign saying, *Built by German prisoner of war, 1917, Halifax, N.S.* Whenever he found her staring at it, he'd never understood her. *It's so strange, trying to imagine the man who built it*, she'd said once, and he just mocked her, *Next you'll be daydreaming about the carpenter who pounded in the nails of the house*. Why had he said that, laughing, so she dropped her gaze? How could he withdraw or undo the mockery? He had other such moments just as small festering like sores in his memory.

When the modelling session was over and he slowly got dressed, he wished the sketching had gone on longer into the night. Then, pulling on his coat, he turned to one of the easels and saw what someone had made of him: a knobby-limbed old man, sour-mouthed, sexless, a hand proudly cupping a knee, the pose pathetically rigid, ridiculous.

"High time for a rest, don't you think?" Bent over to him, Carmen straightened the blankets, brushed his cheek with her mitten. They'd pulled up against the edge of the canal, near a wooden bench, a lamp hanging from a curved black pole. His head propped in his hand, he watched Percy twisting the top off the thermos, steam escaping in a ghostly plume. When Carmen pulled the filled thermos cup away from Percy and whispered, "Let him drink first," he glanced at the distant lights of houses, ashamed that she thought he needed coffee more than she or Percy did. Clutching the plastic handle, he lifted the cup to his lips.

He almost spat out the liquid – it wasn't coffee, but hot chocolate, mild-tasting hot chocolate. His nose had been too plugged to smell the difference. As he braced himself, he vowed not to breathe a word of complaint, and drank heartily. He'd also keep quiet about his cold feet and his itching knee. A church bell was ringing – why at that hour, on a week night? – its peals flying past houses and across streets, adding a further hardness to the frigid February air.

Carmen whispered something to Percy.

The hot chocolate had made the rounds once, then when she returned to him and handed him a cookie she said, "We've got something to tell you." Her voice shook and her lips looked tight. Percy was sitting in the background, tightening his laces. "We thought you should know, we're moving out the first of May."

The news was what he'd guessed, so he just lay there blank-faced and bit into the cookie. Carob chips – he hated the taste. *The first of May.* Then he would be alone with Julie. She would be in her housecoat at the dining room table, silent, with piles of paperwork in front of her, her hand rubbing the back of her neck.

"We found a house for ourselves," Carmen said, her back to him as she returned to the bench. "We didn't want to say anything until we were sure."

Percy pulled at his beard. "With another bambino on the way, we need more space."

"Space," Carmen echoed. "You don't know how sick we are of living in that basement."

He spat the cookie into the snow and felt a dribble down his chin. He'd never sensed more sharply that Dr. Pack was right – he'd sold the kennels and left home mostly to "bury his grief," to escape from an emptiness impossible to imagine before. What if it had all been a mistake, a much bigger mistake than his agreeing to the bone-shaking, nerve-rattling toboggan ride along the canal? He doubted if he had the energy or the courage – or whatever it would take – to move back east.

He pulled the blankets up to his chin, turned away from Carmen and Percy, and shut his eyes. Half of him might've been floating overhead in the night sky, suspended like some dark kite, looking down at himself. "You didn't have to bring me all the way down here," he said, "just to tell me that." The whole toboggan-on-the-ice idea now seemed a lie, a trick. He was tempted to let out a choked groan. He did.

"Are you trying to make us feel like rats for doing this?" Carmen asked. "Jesus, Gramp – you're not being fair – think of us." Sounds of crunching snow, sighing, muttering. She must've been hobbling on her skates back towards him. He opened his eyes and saw her earrings glint above him. One of those punks on the bus had worn earrings.

"Take me home," he said, "before this rattles all my teeth loose."

"Jesus, Gramp," Carmen repeated. "What're we supposed to do?"

Percy's skates hitting the ice. The tug of the toboggan. The rope shaking, sweeping snow out of the way.

Back out in the middle of the canal, fewer skaters raced past. His legs felt sluggish as if both were in casts. His nose was running again in the cold but he didn't bother with his handkerchief, with having to loosen and rearrange the blankets again. The Irish setter trotted past, alone, no master in sight. He gathered his strength, lifted his head towards the round moon, and saw Ramses' daughter, then Amelia. He wanted to pretend she saw him too. *Did I touch you all the ways you wanted to be touched?* Then – startling – lower down he found the Parliament buildings lit into greenish tints, fading into darkness like a postcard of the Nation's Capital blurring underwater. *Why was your laugh so quiet?* He could see himself climbing off election trains, waving at crowds, touching or shaking strangers' hands. If he could imagine that – going into politics – could he imagine for himself any life he hadn't lived? He gripped one of his crutches as if he dared not let go of it. *What did you feel when you first saw me skating?* The toboggan shook and shuddered, clattered and groaned, louder and louder. They were taking him back to the car, the house, the kitchen, the carpeted stairs, to the bedroom with ships floating in blue wallpaper.

JUDITH KALMAN

Not for Me a Crown of Thorns

"Come down," Sári hissed at her sister Cimi, glancing back at the white stuccoed house. Anyone stepping from the cook's entrance to the outhouse at the end of the verandah would notice the elm's trembling branches. Rózsa the cook, looking out the window over her broad, pine-planked counter, might glimpse a yellow hairbow winking through the elm's flame-shaped leaves. Pulling her hands from the bread dough, she'd descend on them in a trice, surprisingly agile despite her girth and shuffling slippers. More often than not she could spring from one side of the big kitchen to the other to smack away the fingers of one of the seven children – even the grown ones – anticipating the hand that would stealthily approach the cheesecloth covering her freshly baked *béles*.

When Sári and Cimi were little, Rózsa struck like lightning if they toddled into the path of the servant girl as she hauled a vat of steaming laundry off the wood-stoked stove. Little one screaming in the clutch of Rózsa's elbow and Rózsa shrieking too that now she had to do the work of the Fraulein! Poor mistress, if she only knew the peril that stalked her brood, but better she was spared so she could preside in the shop with patience and grace. Rózsa liked to feel in charge. After all, it was she who prepared the first solids to pass the lips of each of the babies, even the eldest, she who held the choicest morsels to their pink satin mouths, feeding them like birdlings from her hand. The Fraulein taught the babies to take food off a spoon, but it was

Rózsa's privilege to give them the best bits from her thick red fingers. Automatically she would silence the startled toddler with a tidbit from her counter.

"Get down *now*!" Sári commanded her sister, who had leapt into the tree without thinking.

"Did you hear! I know it's up there, poor little thing, and now it can't get back."

Before Sári could retort, "It's a cat. That's what cats do, they climb," Cimi had tucked her dress into her knickers and melted into the thick foliage of the elm's lowest boughs. They would be lucky if it was only Rózsa who caught them. Wiping her hands on her apron as she waddled across the lawn, she would instinctively reach up into the tree and yank Cimi by the foot before she had gotten far. "Have you lost your senses?" she'd demand, giving Cimi a light cuff. "Don't you realize your Apuka will be home from the field at any moment?" But Cimi didn't realize anything when an impulse overcame her. Sári itched to go after her and give her plait a good tug.

"You'll be sorry, you will, when Apuka gets hold of you," she threatened, but with little comfort because she knew she would catch it too. Her father, losing his head in terror, would hold her responsible for letting her sister climb. It made her so cross, the unfairness of it. *She* hadn't chased the cat up the tree.

At this very moment Apuka might be turning off the main road that led into town from the vineyards, his light coat draped over his shoulder, his head hatted like any decent Jew, but not the flat round hat of the highly orthodox. His was contemporary and business-like with a deep front V and a brim he pinched as he greeted an acquaintance. Apuka had little patience for the traditions of the devout. If they lost themselves in the scriptures and let their children starve, why shouldn't the world also believe it had a right to sweep them aside? As for the rich and holier-than-thou who scattered charitable disbursements in hopes of buying a seat in heaven, perhaps they believed the Lord's ear, too, might be purchased?

Apuka had no use for those who showed off their faith, any more than he had for morning, afternoon, and evening prayers. A blessing for the fruit of the earth, yes naturally. As for the rest, let the *yeshiva bochers* who came begging for their meals at the cook's entrance put in a few extra words for him. He wasn't ashamed to ask or to slip a coin into their pockets. He was a busy man. What else had *they* to do?

Sári snickered, remembering the poor rabbinical student last week who had entered through the kitchen and been engulfed in the rich odours that built up after Rózsa had been in the kitchen from daybreak. Something still baked in the great, wood-stoked oven, and soup steamed and steeped on the range. Rózsa ordered him to the table piled high with bowls and cutlery, pointing a red arm bared by her rolled-up sleeve, so the shame-faced student had to avert his eyes. While he squirmed uncomfortably, he heard voices raised in the other rooms, and then someone's skirts swished past him and out the door. Girls moved in and out to pick up clean washing or tear chunks from the loaves that lined the counter. He was afraid to raise his head lest he glimpse the pale flesh under an arm that reached up to fix a hairpin. By the time the servant girl had cleared him a place and pushed a bowl under his nose, he was too overwhelmed to eat.

"*Nu* –" Apuka's hard elbow poked him in the back. "Does the Lord forbid even a bite of bread? Eat or you won't grow a beard long enough for the anti-Semites to yank."

While the girls tittered, Apuka bent down to whisper, "No harm will take you here. *This* is not the devil's camp." And, as usual, pressed a few clammy coins into the young man's fingers.

If Sári and Cimi were lucky, Apuka would be stalled a few moments along the way home by someone he knew. Well, business could always be better, but he daren't complain. As long as there was food on the table.

Food on the table and stores in the larder, chickens in the yard, and fruit from his vines. Five beautiful daughters and two smart-mouthed sons, he mustn't seem ungrateful for the bounty of the Lord, nor dare he boast lest he tempt the evil eye. Apuka was shrewd and superstitious. Spitting into the dirt to ward off ill-intentioned hexes, he would tip his hat and continue home for his midday meal.

When he came in from the field, he was usually in good humour. The store put him out of sorts. If a child had a desire or appeal, now was the time to present it. Apuka was best approached while the outdoor air still filled his lungs, before he turned to town and the affairs of the shop. Rózsa would have cleared the sink of crockery for the master's arrival. Pumping the handle above the deep basin as Apuka rinsed what he called the "clean dirt" of the fields from his hands, the child would present his or her request. This was when Apuka felt most disposed to listen to the hankerings of his children: a few *filér* for the "useless cinema" the older ones frequented, or the porcelain-headed doll one of the girls had set her heart on but which in the fall, after being shut in at the shop for days on end, he would threaten to burn with the leaves, "as if there aren't enough bodies underfoot in this house already!" It would go especially hard for them, Sári thought, to disrupt Apuka's midday peace.

She looked up into the tree's twitching branches. Its thick foliage spread over her like a green sky dotted with stars of sunlight so sharp she had to squint. Cimi's legs above her drooped indolently. Anyone glancing from the house would notice the dangling legs without knowing exactly whose they were. After all, both little girls from that house ran around naked-legged in the sunshine save for the white ankle socks on their sandalled feet. It incensed her to be implicated in Cimi's offence. The cat wasn't hers. Like all cats it had attached itself to Cimi.

In the nursery last night, the kitten seemed hardly more than a balled-up sock, or a pom-pom that might hang on the tie of a fur-trimmed hood.

"Shut up," Cimi had warned her before she could protest the presence of a cat in their bed and alert Fraulein to another flouting of the household's rules. "It's too little to have any fleas yet. Just look at it."

Sári ran a finger along the delicate spine of the kitten. Its grey fur was meltingly soft, like the downy head of a baby. It was impossibly sweet – but already Cimi's. It nestled only in the crook of Cimi's skinny arm. Cimi was a charmer of felines. She had but to breathe on a cat and it would let her do anything – wrap its head in a doll's bonnet and stuff it into a pram. They sheathed their claws for Cimi.

"Get down here, stupid," Sári ordered again, her throat sore from the strain of whispering.

"I heard it just this minute," Cimi called, not even trying to pipe down. "I'm sure I'll find it, but you're no help."

"Idiot," Sári muttered. Idiotic and headstrong and thought-less. Sári would have to go up there to silence her before Apuka would hear.

She put a dainty foot on the bark of the tree, feeling for the familiar knot she braced herself against when she mounted. They had all climbed that tree, each child in his and her time. But never under Apuka's nose. Like the others she was an able climber. Maybe not quite such a monkey as Cimi, who could shimmy up effortlessly. But then neither was Sári such a stupid goat as to run headlong into resistance. There was no budging Apuka on the subject of trees, not even such a healthy and ven-erable one as this elm with so many branches you could climb it like a ladder. They had each of them tried at least once to per-suade him.

"Apuka dearest, it's such a safe tree – look at it," they pleaded. "All those sturdy branches so close together. You'd have to be crippled not to climb it."

"Bite your tongue," Apuka thundered, and his hand flew up as though to strike them but hovered, instead, above his own head. "You don't know what you're talking about. Your Mamuka's brother he was a big shot, ya, a know-it-all like you. But he fell out of a tree. Just once!" At this point Apuka raised his other hand and joined the two in a hard smack. "And that was that."

To climb in full view, when Apuka was due home from the shack in the fields they called his "office" – the base from which he supervised the field hands and met with buyers who wanted to inspect his crop – to climb at midday was like butting your head into a wall.

"Goat – stupid, stubborn, wilful," Sári seethed as she craned to see where Cimi had clambered.

She'd go up there and give Cimi a piece of her mind. She had the nerve, getting Sári into trouble like this. Sári knew better.

There were many ways to get what you wanted. Apuka was home only for an hour or two at midday. They could have had all afternoon to look for the cat. Sári's mouth pursed grimly as she followed her sister.

Once when they were little, Cimi had nearly disfigured her. Early on, Sári's features had shown promise of her older sisters' mild beauty. A natural dowry would be useful when she grew up, fourth of five sisters. She had quickly learned to value and exploit her appearance. Mamuka used the best fabrics from the shop to fashion their outfits. Even the boys were her mannequins. The children's charming features and Mamuka's handsome garments made the best billboard for the wares of the shop. But then there was Cimi, mercurial and unthinking, who one *Pesach*, dressed in holiday velvet, had refused to wait patiently on the front yard lawn while Mamuka buttoned the endless rows on the other children's frocks and jackets. Cimi had wandered away and ruined her vestments in the shitpile down the road. That was Cimi for you. And on that other occasion, Cimi left Sári with a permanent scar.

It was just a chance that the brick she had thrown had caught Sári's hairline. The madness of Cimi, not more than four or five at the time, Apuka's old fedora flopping over her eyes. When she had tipped back the hat, her eyes flared icy blue in fury. Then she levelled them in deadly aim at her bossy sister.

"This is one time too many you've made me be the Father!"

Sári was transfixed by the flash storm that transformed her tender-hearted and usually obliging sister. She froze, spellbound, watching the brick lurch in her direction. Blood ran warm wet down her face, spilling onto Mamuka's old gown that bespoke Sári's role as Mother. Cimi stared at her hand as though it had a deviant will of its own. When Sári realized, outraged, that she had been struck by her sister, she gasped from the pain in her forehead, wind slicing exposed flesh. They were just a year apart, raised like twins, the last of the litter. Both of them were amazed at this rupture that oozed sticky and red between them. The shock of it silenced them. It took Rózsa's arrival and then the Fraulein's to restore howls and commotion to the scene.

Sári's legs pumped purposefully up the rungs of the elm. How often must she be threatened by the thoughtlessness of her sister? There was that other time too, Rózsa's gleaming gutting knife poised in Cimi's fingers: "There's going to be a funeral around here Miss Schoolteacher *Sarah*," she'd spat because Sári had tried to crown her with a duncecap.

This time Sári was going to stop Cimi in her tracks before Sári had to pay the price.

"Where are you? I'm coming," she hissed up into the branches.

"Shh," Cimi answered from closer than Sári had expected. "Listen, I think I hear something." She had straddled a limb above Sári on the other side of the trunk.

"I don't care," Sári said, joining her, "We can get it later. We may still have time to get down before Apuka sees."

"What? Do you think he'll climb up to get us? Besides, he doesn't have to notice. We'll go down after he leaves."

"Don't be stupid," Sári snapped. "We can't stay up here forever. You better come down now before you get any more bright ideas."

"You think you know everything, don't you?" Cimi flicked a braid over her shoulder, catching Sári on the cheek. "Shut up. I'm sure I heard it, poor little pet."

Cimi pulled herself to her feet. Balancing her fingers against the trunk, she slid along the branch until she got a clearer view. Then she stretched her other arm into the leaves overhead. The branch dipped from the weight of her movements, and Sári had a brief premonition of vertigo as she watched Cimi grope blindly at the ungraspable air.

"Watch it," she admonished, forgetting not to care. "It's only a cat." But Sári knew it couldn't be *only* a cat to Cimi. If it breathed, it was blessed.

The plaintive mewing of a kitten could be heard faintly through the rustling leaves. Well, that sealed it. There would be no getting Cimi down until the cat was in hand.

Cimi let go the trunk and sidled further along the limb, making soothing noises to the kitten. "There, there, kitty, here I come." Sári boiled with agitation. What if Cimi the fool slipped?

It wasn't fair that Cimi should upset her so. She had no right to be so reckless and sure of herself. She was so selfish, not even thinking how Sári might feel stuck up here, unable to do anything but watch and worry. For *she* wasn't such an idiot as to startle Cimi now, or get her into an argument. *She* wasn't one to imperil her sister.

"There!" Cimi had leapt up like a gymnast, and now swung from the overhead branch.

"Stop it! Right now!" Sári shouted, unable to prevent herself from raising her voice. "Now! Do you hear me, Cimi! You get back here now!"

Cimi's legs swayed above the limb she had balanced on, and she inched her palms towards the thinning edge of the branch overhead. Then, in a swift move that forced Sári's heart into her mouth, she let go her right hand and grabbed at thin air. Sári saw something grey explode from the leaves while Cimi's legs scissored.

"Idiot!" she yelled, but Cimi had already swung back to the trunk and dropped like a cat herself to the limb below. Around her neck the kitten clung like a fur collar.

"So who's stupid now?" Cimi grinned.

"Down! Both of you! Down here!" their father's voice cracked through the golden noon light. He choked out the order. From the girls' perch they saw his fist raised against them, and behind it his upturned twisted face.

Apuka's passions played through his body as through an instrument. He had a quick, impatient mind that expressed itself in neuralgic aches and pains, headaches, a delicate stomach. His terror of heights translated into rage.

"Get down. Brats. Disobedient wretches. Get what you deserve!"

The tree shook and shuddered around Sári, alive with a swift wind. Cimi, kitten clutching her shoulder, had taken flight and was climbing again, impossibly higher.

"Cimi! Sárika!" a chorus called from the foot of the tree. Rózsa, red-faced and wringing her hands in her apron. Háni the girl, gazing up blankly until Rózsa slapped her awake to send her running, Sári presumed, to fetch Mamuka from the shop. Looking down from her roost she noticed that her quick-tongued brother Laci was chewing ruminatively on lunch, hands in the pockets of his short pants. Fraulein skipped up finally, calling their names as though she had been searching for them this long while. She'd feel a guilty twinge or two before this was over, Sári gloated. Toni, their eldest sister, graceful as a willow, leaned gently towards the elm, hand shielding her eyes from the glare. Cimi shouted at them all from aloft: "You can't make me!"

And now Sári too joined the fracas. "Stupid. Don't be so stupid. It's just a spanking!"

She strained her eyes up into the shaking branches where, instead of spying Cimi, she was assaulted by the sun's stabbing rays. White and blinding they pierced through the leaves, striking Sári and obliterating her sister. When she glanced down again at the gathering of her kin they were sprayed by sun spots that left brilliant holes in their chests, bellies, and eyes. She was stunned by the blasted peace of the noontime idyll. The green and gold canopy that had sheltered two little girls and a baby kitten, the dangling of skinned knees and sagging socks and braids the colour of milk chocolate shattered like a picture in glass.

Sári was paralysed, bewildered. Alone in the tree, she felt bereft of all that rooted her. A weightlessness filled her head. The earth moved ever so slightly as though she might lift off and spin like a balloon on a current of air. She could pass out of this world now, lift, and drift away. She would be spared living out her searing vision of the future.

"Sar-i-*ka*!" Rózsa's scream pierced her reverie, making her grab the tree trunk. Rózsa – red-faced, heavy, stout of heart, knew Sári and her siblings better than she knew her own children who ranged in the fields around the shanty that was their home outside of town. She had noticed Sári waver, and insisted on life at any cost: "You'll be sorry, Miss, if I have to come up there to get you!"

How had she gotten into this, Sári wondered, dazed by the fear of those below and the dangerous flight overhead of her sister. She was a good girl. She hadn't gone looking for trouble.

"Nitwits," Laci laughed up at them, "are you going to climb up to the sun?"

Well, Cimi might think she could escape forever, but Sári knew what was really possible. She descended reluctantly, regretting with each footfall the decline of her role in the drama.

Too stiff with panic to cast about for a switch, or loosen his belt, Apuka beat her with his bare hand. Face smeared with tears and snot, head upside down because she was bent over, Sári barely made out the grey blur that streaked into the grass a moment before Apuka pushed her away so he could spring after her sister. Feckless, sly Cimi had waited until Apuka was absorbed in the beating, then scrambled down the tree trunk and sprinted off.

"Cimi, get back here!"

But Cimi ran and ran, her legs toughened by climbing trees and dodging the boys from the Christian Fathers' Lycée, who tried to pull her braids and worse if they could catch her. Apuka staggered home puffing, his shirt soaked with sweat, hand on his heaving chest. Mamuka waited with some stitching in her lap. Deploring the spectacle they had made of themselves, Mamuka sat stitching, her mouth pressed tight.

Sári barely noticed the shadows lengthen along the nursery floorboards. All afternoon she lay on the bed, face stuffed into her pillow. Voices, low and conciliatory, wafted from the main room where Mamuka had spread her sewing on the divan that pulled out nightly for the older girls' bed. Tonight there would be no guests invited to sip cordials and enjoy the big girls' renditions of operetta numbers. The young ones, lying two by two in the nursery, wouldn't keep each other awake with scary stories about the one-legged beggar who prowled the streets of the Jewish quarter. There would be no pauses to listen to laughter ripple from the adjacent room when their sisters finished a popular song, and no succumbing to giggles that made the Austrian Fraulein get up time and again muttering her guttural hushes. The household was still in the aftermath of its midday crisis. It was quiet with implied recriminations and apologies.

Sári heard the subdued sounds of the household as though from miles away. They had abandoned her and left her to her misery. Nobody cared. When Apuka came back sweating and panting, he had tried to take her in his arms.

"It's all over now, Sárika darling. You're home and safe."

But she had shaken free. Over for him, perhaps, now that he didn't need to worry. But what about her? No one seemed to care that she had been unfairly punished.

"Really, Sumi." Mamuka's grey eyes widened when she saw Apuka so dishevelled. It was enough to quell him and drive him to the pump where he scooped water over his neck. Sári, sticky and sopping, waited in the door for consolation. She had been beaten and humiliated, but Mamuka only wiped Sári's face with her lace handkerchief and sat her down at the table with a glass of water. Sári stared into the glass, tears welling. It wasn't fair. She had been dutiful. She'd only gone up into the tree to fetch Cimi down. She hadn't run away and given Apuka a pain in his side. No one felt the slightest bit sorry for the wrong Sári had suffered. Her tears fell into the glass, and turned to sobs.

"Sárika," Mamuka sighed. "You know you gave your father such a fright."

Fright! Her fright had been worse. She'd been subjected to Cimi's acrobatics in the air. What if Apuka had seen that! His fright was nothing compared to hers, but no one took her feelings into account. Sári put her hand on her heart and sobbed even harder.

"What's this," Laci teased, "is someone beating you again?"

Such an insult, to have her misery made light of.

In the end there was nothing for it but to let Rózsa lift Sári in her big arms and carry her, legs trailing limply, to bed in the nursery.

She conjured sorrowful scenarios that stoked her tears. How sorry they all would be when she died of her broken heart. Her brief, tender life sacrificed by a cruel family. Then they would be exposed for their heartlessness. Cimi would be banished for the trouble she had made. She would get her reward finally for all the wrongs she had inflicted on her blameless sister. They would cast Cimi out of the family fold. When no one was looking, after the funeral cortege had finished its bitter business of burying Sári's lifeless, beautiful body, Cimi would crawl out from among the cemetery willows like a cast-out cur, and throw herself weeping on Sári's grave.

The sad and gratifying image entertained Sári through the long afternoon.

Too restless to coop himself up at the shop after an unnaturally quiet lunch, Apuka drifted out onto the back lawn. He gazed up at the huge elm and wondered how he had come to dread it. The elm had been here long before he had brought his bride to the house not even a decade into the century, more than twenty years ago. The house had appealed to him because of its proximity to the road that led from Beregszász's Jewish quarter to the vineyards and groves of the surrounding countryside. In the days of his father, the land had been Russian. Sometimes Russian, sometimes Magyar or Austro-Hungarian. In any case they had remained Jews, whoever was master. Like the tree, they were rooted here and fixed in place.

When Apuka had brought his bride to the whitewashed, single-storey structure that would be their home, the tree seemed to him to guard its back flank like a sentinel. So solid and enduring, he felt lucky. Was it a surprise, then, that the children responded to its outstretched, beckoning boughs? At that time the house consisted of two commodious chambers, the kitchen and the main room that served for everything else. They had entered through the main room's portal at the front of the house and surveyed its generous proportions. Now the door was permanently blocked by the walnut chiffonnier that held drawers of table linens. And the two rooms had grown to four.

Tentatively Apuka touched the bark. It was just a tree, beautiful, shapely, a green fact he used to take comfort in when he left the house at dawn through the kitchen entrance. He would glance at the tree dominating his yard and think, yes, it was anchored here. Whatever ill wind might blow through, it would hold firm. Inside the house his family slept. Rózsa would arrive presently to begin their first meal. The family had burgeoned, requiring first a nursery addition, then spilling into the main room and raising the need for a chamber for the parents. The rooms opened one into the other. On the previous night, when the lights were extinguished in the main room, Mamuka and Apuka had passed through the nursery that breathed with the syncopated rhythms of the babies, to their own room that was small but luxurious in its privacy. The newel-posted bed looked weighted by silk eiderdowns and goose-feathered pillows in monogrammed slipcovers. He'd marvelled at how quickly their children had sprung into the world. The bed had spawned five girls and two boys in hardly a dozen years.

Sometimes the thought of all his children overwhelmed Apuka. He'd grow restless and anxious, especially during long afternoons in the shop. The role of shopkeeper didn't suit him. When he tried to be pleasant, he appeared ingratiating. Mamuka was the genius behind the store's success. Somehow she managed to flatter her customers at no expense to her personal dignity. She was gracefully persuasive.

In the shop, Apuka filled with pent-up energy and worried about his family's welfare. Each child had added exponentially to the quantity and variety of ills that might befall them. The boys were indeed bright and the girls pleasing to look at; they had been endowed the wherewithal to secure their future. But he was plagued with misgivings. During Mamuka's childhood, her brother had fallen from a tree and died. More recently, Sárika's best friend was crippled by polio. And now there were suitors who came calling for his eldests, some from faraway towns where Apuka had no connections. How was he to know which strangers would secure them a good life?

Mamuka's disapproval of his outburst made him doubt himself. These days if Apuka came to think of it, the tree filled him with foreboding. There was a kind of treachery in its massive, unwieldy bulk. The thing was trapped by its roots, ingrown as much as it was growing. And it could snatch from him what was most precious in its high ensnaring fingers. The tree's permanence didn't strike him as reassuring. Instead, it made him feel bound to this place simply because he knew no other.

Shadows collected on the lawn, but Apuka could still feel the heat of the summer sun in the warm bark of the tree. It passed into his palm. They were rooted here, he and the elm. Was that good for his children? When he imagined them up in the high branches of the tree, he panicked. He saw them, light-boned and delicate, singing their modern songs as guilelessly as birds. What if an ill wind were to blow through? A wind dark and fierce with malice, that blew them away to the ends of the earth? Apuka chided himself. Here he was in his own yard, holding the sun's heat in his hands, yet worrying over something unlikely. He'd better find something more fruitful to do.

All the while, Cimi lounged along a thick bough overhead, looking down at her father. He seemed too subdued. The odd way he touched the tree made her uncomfortable. Apuka wasn't given to moody reflection. He was active and opinionated and as likely to burst into song as one of his children. What was he doing communing with a tree trunk? She wanted to distract him. Poor Apuka, to be so troubled over a big old tree that was as sturdy and safe as the ground. It felt queer to be sorry for her father. She was more accustomed to Apuka's flash rages. Those she knew how to handle. Why, all she had to do was lead him on a chase. Eventually he would tire of his anger. Today she had circled back to the yard after shaking Apuka off her scent, then taken refuge where no one would think she'd have the audacity to hide.

Because she was in the tree again, she hesitated from calling down, even though Apuka looked sad and in need of comfort. For the first time Cimi regretted having provoked her father. She must have upset him a great deal, she thought, to cause him to hang about like this. Poor Apuka to be so needlessly worked up. She and her siblings were as sure-footed as mountain goats. The tree was like a second home. She had lain on the branch all afternoon, idly breaking off twigs and leaves, and working them in her fingers until she found she could twine them together. As she fashioned the sticks and flakes of bark into something that had shape, she forgot all about the time despite the gnawing in her tummy. When Apuka came outside, she was just beginning to notice that the sun's rays had faded.

"Apuka," she risked calling as he turned away. "Apuka, wait!"

The sound of Cimi's voice pulled Apuka's heartstrings. Fool, he was as sentimental as he was hot-tempered. Soon he would get teary-eyed like his daughters over a popular ballad. Here came Cimi scrambling down the tree trunk and he felt like the thing had taken pity on him, returning his youngest, wildest bird. Well, let this be a lesson to him to stop brooding and count his blessings.

"There you are, you bad child. You better come in and have a word with your sister," he said, holding out his arms to her.

Cimi was sorry about Sári's spanking but it was Sári's own fault that she hadn't tried to get away. She was always telling Cimi what to do as though she knew everything, but look what it had gotten her. Cimi knew Sári would blame her, and Sári could be unforgiving. Well – she nestled contentedly in Apuka's arms – it wouldn't hurt to beg Sári's pardon. Cimi, after all, had escaped.

"What have you got there?" asked Apuka, noticing the circlet in her hand.

"See," she said playfully, "I've made you a crown."

He laughed proudly, noting the clever way she had worked the rough, hard wood of the elm. His children weren't just beautiful. They were clever and talented, blessed with the gifts of the Lord.

"That will never get around my thick skull," Apuka patted Cimi. "You must wear it yourself."

Sári stirred from her pool of misery when she heard them come in. The creak of the kitchen door plucked her attention. It was about time Cimi made an appearance and got what she deserved.

"So," pronounced Rózsa heavily, "the prodigal comes home."

A moment's hesitation hung in the air.

"On Apuka's shoulders? More like the conquering hero."

Laci's saucy rejoinder broke the tension. Led by Mamuka's barely suppressed chortle, the family erupted in laughter.

Sári felt she'd been smacked. They *laughed* about what Cimi did? To relieve the strain of the long quiet afternoon, they were willing to overlook Cimi's offence?

"Yes!" Cimi chirped, quick to capitalize on the mood, "I even have a laurel wreath like Caesar!"

Sári froze in outrage. Now Cimi evidently was showing off something the others greeted with delight. With just a wise-crack and some trinket, she had dispelled the afternoon's solemnity. Was that how cheaply justice could be bought? Sári felt violated. Cimi had injured her *again*, but everyone ignored it. The shock staunched her tears and withered her self-pity. She felt walled off from her family by her sense of what was right. Sári was the good child. Didn't that count for anything?

Softly the nursery door opened, and light flooded the doorway. Cimi's slight figure seemed to drown in it. Some hero, Sári scoffed – tiny, bird-boned, and wearing on her head an ugly, twiggy thing, no doubt the work of "art" Cimi had used to charm their family. Sári was disgusted with them for being so easily duped.

"What do you want," Sári demanded. Cimi didn't approach right away, but floated in the portal. When she stepped into the room's darkness, it looked from Sári's position in bed that Cimi's feet plunged through the light. With each step towards Sári, Cimi sank further.

Fifteen years later Sári remembered this impression of her sister sinking until finally all Sári really noticed was the twiggy thing on Cimi's head. A moment before Cimi was to commit her wildest, rashest act, Sári remembered her head festooned like a bramble of briers.

The *kapo* assigned to their block in Auschwitz was crazy, everyone could see that. Maybe that's what it did to you when you tormented your own kind. He was a Jew, but his authority maddened him against them. If their hair wasn't shaved he would have clutched and torn it while addressing any one of them. His hatred wasn't specific. He satisfied himself with kicking them in the ribs to make them get up. The weakest among them inflamed his fury; a bruise was invitation for him to beat it again. Perhaps he saw them as fuel for the furnace. If not for his rage, he might end up there himself.

Sári didn't know when exactly Cimi took leave of her senses. It was an inexorable progression like the other separations: the forcible expulsion from their home and splitting up of the family. Apuka and his sons-in-law were dragged off with the men. Mercifully, Laci and their older brother had left the country for university before the worst was upon them. But Mamuka and the older girls – the older sisters and their babies – were taken from the main block and never seen again. Now there were only Sári and Cimi left. Sári didn't notice the first signs of Cimi's absence. Her blue eyes had flattened, her arms hung limp. But all of them in the camp were vacant to some extent.

It took a while for Sári to come out of herself enough to notice a change in Cimi. Ordered to file in, she'd tug Cimi along. In the queue for food, she poked Cimi to remind her to hold out her tin plate. Eventually Sári found herself thinking more about Cimi than herself. She was almost grateful for the distraction.

Daily, it was getting harder for Sári to keep Cimi going. It occurred to Sári that, squatting over the shitpile, Cimi might actually let her muscles give way and sink into the filth. They would be ordered to bury her in it were such an accident to occur. But Sári knew it would be no mistake. Cimi's withdrawal was as steady as the shuffling advance of the queue that snaked towards the showers.

Leaning against the wooden shell of the barrack, Cimi's jaw slackened. She could sit immobile and in such complete absence from her body, the spit would collect at the corner of her mouth. When no one was looking, Sári stroked Cimi's cheek to make its reflex tighten up. But she couldn't work Cimi's muscles for her all the time.

"Idiot!" the kapo shouted, belting Cimi's loose mouth. "Do you know what happens to idiots in this place?"

Cimi didn't flinch. Perhaps she had already abandoned her nerves. Perhaps she'd escaped. Infuriated, the kapo pawed her eyelid, prying it up. "Do you think you can make me believe you're sick?"

He shoved his thumb into her eyeball and pressed, grinding his thumb into the socket until Sári pictured the eye oozing out like the white of an egg. She had floated above the compound, and watched from a plane that prevented her from grabbing the kapo but not from seeing what happened. Sári hovered over the horror that was imminent, and the picture of Cimi long ago came into her mind. Twigs and bark and spiky leaves stuck out from Cimi's hair. The light in the doorway, Sári realized, was flickering lamplight from the main room in which the family was gathered. It flickered and flowed in waves. Cimi broke from the liquid glow in the doorway, and tried to wade towards her. But each footfall sank deeper. Sári tried warning her off.

"Get lost," Sári had threatened. "Leave me alone."

As Sári hovered, recalling the strange image, Cimi hit the kapo. Before he succeeded in blinding her, she hit him in the face. Sári thudded back to the present, her heart beating wildly. Cimi had been gone days, maybe weeks, and when she came to she hit the kapo. She hit him with the back of her hand. *A reflex?* The kind of reflex that made you kick a mad dog that was foaming at the mouth? The kind of reflex that made you climb to the treetop where its branches had thinned to matchsticks? A reflex of defiance or death?

The kapo's blows broke the thin skin on Cimi's skull, and blood poured down her forehead. Blood flowed from everywhere. From her split head and smashed nose and torn cheek. From her battered mouth. Her face was a bloody pulp by the time a German guard stopped the disgusting display.

Sári stuffed her rag of a skirt into Cimi's mouth to stifle the screams that welled now from the place where she'd been hiding. For Cimi had been in hiding. Hiding somewhere in a secret place. Not that far away, but very carefully hidden.

Sári remembered Rózsa, big and red like when Sári and Cimi were little girls, not wasted as she was by the time she and all the rest were taken to be gassed. But Rózsa as she had stood under the elm like a tree herself, an extension of the earth that fed and formed them. Rózsa ordering Sári down from where she had drifted high above the elm: "You'll be sorry, Miss, if I have to come up there to get you!" But Cimi had continued climbing, higher and higher. What happened to the bird Noah sent out first, the one that flew high and wide but didn't return? The premature courier defeated by the flood and dark clouds and not a dry twig in sight. What happened after she was dispatched too soon? Sobbing, Sári stopped Cimi's mouth with her filthy skirt. She held Cimi down as she writhed and bucked in her blood. The bird who couldn't bring herself to return with the terrible news of what she had seen. Only a lunatic kapo could make her do that.

An evening a lost world ago, Cimi had entered the nursery wearing an ugly, spiky thing their family had applauded like a work of art. It made Sári sick. She felt sick that Cimi was rewarded for misbehaving while she had to suffer. She was sick from the unfairness of it. And it made her sick to see how pathetic Cimi looked. Small, skinny, crowned like some martyr, and cruelly drenched in a surfeit of light.

"Sári," Cimi answered meekly, "don't hold it against me that I ran away. What would be the sense of both of us getting thrashed?"

She took off her creation and held it out as a peace offering. "Here. You can have it. I worked on it all afternoon."

Sári didn't know why she was so hard. She was only a child then. Nothing bad had happened to them yet. But her heart was hard and set, and she wouldn't accept such cheap reparation. She would have nothing to do with that wreath her sister had made. Her skin crawled to think of it prickly and poking on her head. She had been beaten and wronged, but not for her the crown of a martyr.

"Keep your stupid crown," Sári said, pushing it away. Then, because Cimi looked crestfallen, Sári relented a little and made room for her in the bed.

"Listen," Cimi whispered after a bit. Sári heard nothing but the usual sounds of the household restored to its evening liveliness.

"Ssh," Cimi whispered again, "listen outside."

Sári tried to block out the near noises, but she couldn't get past her father's voice followed by a tinkle of laughter. She didn't fault herself any more than she faulted the rest of her family for not hearing better. You would have needed the ears of an animal or something not merely human, to hear so soon, and from such a distance, the black wind in the west.

ANDREW MULLINS

The World of Science

Sheila is off somewhere, counting her money, making her plans. The government has seen fit to mete out $180,000 for her study of humping sea elephants, rice rats, swamp rabbits. Something, anyway, reeking of science. Like any husband, I'm happy for her. Since the advent of the new laws, we cheer on the women in our lives as never before, hoping to God they'll do a better job than we did. But like any citizen's, my mind reels at the amount of cash, enough to fill a mattress to bursting, no doubt about it. Sheila's explanations: the fieldwork is costly, the price of machines extortionate, the graduate students blue in the face with ambition, hunger, something. Protective clothing alone can run into the thousands, she tells me. No doubt it can, I say. It's the swamp rabbits' turn, she says. It certainly is, I say. She is wily, my wife, could no doubt reduce the panel of judges to tears as she panhandled on behalf of her beloved rabbits, elephants, rats. Here, take it, take the money, they'd say, for those poor, aggrieved little fellows. You're a bloody saint, is what you are.

So now she's off somewhere, divvying up the funds, dreaming her Jane-Goodall-of-the-Swamp dreams, enlisting the hungry drudges who adhere like newborn kangaroos to the pouch of academia. Somewhere in the swamps, word goes out, the rabbits are revelling, or perhaps they are hiding, for the truth is I haven't a clue what Sheila does to them, whether it's kind or sinister, though my suspicions, I'm afraid to say, sometimes run to the latter.

And me? I'm left with a perfectly good prime rib, roasted to holy perfection, with which I can do *nothing*. There is something wrong with it all, I say to the dog, who is friendly with me tonight on account of the roast. It was not in our dreams, when we plotted out our lives so long ago, to lose our wife to the world of science this way. Neither, though, were the new laws. The after-effects of which have given rise to sharply honed sensitivities of all sorts, like a fresh skin, feelings we never knew we had, epistemological upheaval, just as, no doubt, the lawmakers in their broad wisdom had intended all along. Still, there's the matter of the missing wife.

But who are we to question, who appointed us Scrutinizer General? No one, that's who. So hold your mouth shut and hope for copper pots. Expensive copper pots, courtesy of the sea elephants and the whoring government.

I carve a good slab of the roast for myself, then toss the rest onto the floor for the dog, who can't believe his luck. He will eat until he barfs hooves. Copper pots, I say. Henckels knives. Something, anyway, nice, for me.

At the mall, I find myself overburdened by canvas sacks bulging with leeks, spaghetti squash, grain-fed free-range capons (on special, ranging no more), and so I sit on a bench. Normally, I shop at Legault *et fils*, skilled purveyors of fine foods, but Legault *et fils* are closed on account of death, which has come for Mme Legault in the form of an airborne mould launched from the heating ducts of her home. When I told Sheila of the death of Mme Legault over the phone, she suggested that somewhere out there someone with a grant is at work on saving future victims. How can one argue with that? But it's too late for Mme Legault, who in life cooked a *chaudfroid* of thrushes unmatched in this city. She'll be sorely missed, I told old Legault. She will, she will, he said, the widower's tears mounting in his old French eyes. "The world was once a paradise for me," he said, "and now it is a prison." Legault *fils*, rubbing his father's back, guiding him away behind the cheese counter. I did not let on that I'd had a moment of terror, one of those panic-laden flashes where you witness the potential for your own grief in the bereavement of another. The loss of Sheila, for instance, bitten by a monkey, that would be more than I could bear.

So while they bury Mme Legault, I am at the mall, sitting on the bench, catching my breath. I am accosted by a small child.

Hi, it says cheerily. A girl of about four, blonde tousled hair, pink mouth like a jujube, eyes like burst litchis.

Hi, I say.

Are you one of the home-daddies? it says.

That I am, I say.

What's that? it says, pointing.

Leeks, I say. For the *soupe à la bonne femme.*

Where are your babies? it says.

Out, in the city, getting their heads pierced by a brute named Carmine, I say. Giant rings through their heads. They are grown-up teenagers, caught in the flourish of adolescent life, not like you, small and fresh. The rings are like haloes. Shining around the heads of the children in the night.

No they're not, it says.

No, I say, you're right. They're not. Not at all.

This is a smart one. I lie to children all the time. I like to think it amuses their small uncharted minds.

I think I've been lost, the child says. My daddy was buying me grapes. He probably lost me. Again.

I feed it a kumquat, watch the look of surprise on its face. It climbs onto my neck. Children will do this, if you let them. It is the conquering instinct they all harbour, deep in their tiny little souls. Giddyup, it says. I take it to the pens, where the lost fathers are reunited with their lost children.

My name is Jennie, it says.

My name, I say, is Pete.

The father appears, red-faced, festooned with grocery bags.

Grapes! says the child.

I get on the bus. The Plymouth is in the shop, being attended to by various grease monkeys, who will perform arcane acts of healing on the vehicle and charge me handsomely for it, drinking all the while from their tubs of Wild Turkey, guzzling from their king cans of Bud. There are things the new laws can't change, no matter how stringently applied, there are constants in the universe, immutable, immaculate. Meanwhile, I ride the bus, the driver of which is a woman, singing Arabic melodies as she drives. The passengers are fascinated by the strange melodies unravelling from the woman's throat, like chains of flowers, like strands of golden thread, like rivulets of mercury rolling through the desert, like a choir of children leaping from the moon. No one will get off the bus, the bus driver stopping at the stops, letting more and more people on, while the old ladies at the front watch their streets go by, Sycamore, Kensington, Winchester Drive.

It's all very different, of course. Who's ever heard of a bus driver who sings (outside of the odd, church-happy Baptist behind the wheel of a school bus)? They used to be big angry men, the bus drivers, primed for a strike at any moment. They'd boot you in the ass as soon as look at you. But that was before the new laws. Now they sing, the ranks of the public transit users swell, some say the ozone is repairing itself. The legislative tribunals say See? See? and I go home, prepare quails with cherries, sit and wait for Sheila.

Sometimes she shows me photographs of carcasses, ice bears, sand cats, ocelots. Something, anyway, in advanced dissection, pinned with railroad spikes to a flatbed truck, ice picks to a butcher block, thumbtacks to a dishtowel, whatever. I don't know where they come from, what they're for, but it's always a reminder there's a good chance I've married a sadist, a bloody Bluebeard, who probably scalps kittens and blinds chimpanzees. I imagine for her a childhood of exploding frogs and drowned beetles. When asked what she does, I don't say she wreaks holy havoc on unfortunate members of the animal world, I don't even know if it's true, can't bear to ask, but sometimes it seems that way. *What did your wife do today?* Eviscerated a gnu, cut a manatee in half.

Not that I don't love her. And not that we don't have our good times. A few weeks ago (before the grant) she pushed me up against the Jenn-Air, bit me in the chest, her hands riffling. Within minutes I was protoplasm. She's a take-charge woman.

That would scare some men. That would send some men packing. But not me, no ma'am. I'm fully secure, tight as all hell with
my own masculine nature. I've been on the wild-man weekends,
swum in the stench of other men, been anointed a grizzly by a
hairy-faced, stick-wielding poet. I came home, tied Sheila to
the bed, prepared a *pêches dame blanche*, and carpeted her with
the stuff. She was almost epileptic, my finger on the button, my
mouth navigating the tableau of peaches, chantilly cream. She
digs it. Science, she says when in these moods, is not the be-all
and end-all.

   Amen to that.

One of the children stands in the living room, abominating me
for crimes of the past, committed, he says, by men of my ilk,
something he's been learning about at the school. A litany of
heinousness flows forth from the boy, rank oppression, bloody
despotism, wanton barbarity, the usual line. I admit to it all, as
I've learned to do over the past few years. The yoke I've slung
round his neck, the shame he must live under, is too much for
his fourteen-year-old soul. His team of counsellors at the school
has told him to work on his self-esteem, his self-esteem is in tat-
ters, so he's gone and got his left foot pierced. He's pissing me off,
as children will do. In Chapter 2 of *Reintegration to the Family*,
a book they bestowed on us with the enactment of the new
laws, Dr. Hortense Laliberté writes candidly, "If they're not
driving you to drink at this age, it may be time to worry." I'm
on my fifth Hennessy at this point, not worried in the least. For
there is still the other one.

   The other one will now eat only bean curd and Hu Yao-bang's
Szechuan sauce #2. She is thirteen years old and has a chain that
runs from a ring in her right ear to a meat hook in her nose. She
is forever plugged into her Walkman, listening to her favourite
band, Lymph Node, Ringworm, Pancreatic Spume, something,
anyway, that sounds like Satan passing a kidney stone, like
camels being boiled alive, like the death of an entire country, the
collapse of the sun. Still, it's catchier than what the boy's been
playing lately, a Wiccan Goddess band who shriek Gaelic sheep-
killing songs.

"These are tough days," writes Dr. Hortense Laliberté in Chapter 4 of *Reintegration to the Family*. Tough! I feel like writing her in a letter. Tough! she says. There are only so many damn shapes, Dr. Laliberté, into which bean curd can be cut.

And where is the wife? Who will help me talk to our daughter, losing up to ten pounds a week, death calculated at that rate for the early spring? Who will comfort the son, plagued with nightmares of his father, a cruel blackguard in the days before the new laws? Who will eat the monkfish tails, the morels *à la poulette*, the braised lettuces, the potato quenelles? Tell me that, Dr. Hortense Laliberté. There are days, I say, when books might as well be foot stools.

A member of the Gas Company is at the door, here to read the gasometer. She carries an industrial steel clipboard, some kind of calculator reminiscent of a Game Boy, looks like she could marshal an entire town for evacuation should a gas main threaten to blow. I escort her to the basement, where she interprets the numbers, feeding them into her Game Boy with considerable aplomb.

"You use a lot of gas," she says.

It's the stove, I tell her. Just this morning I've prepared an *omelette à la ménagère*, *Pommes Impératrice*, *tartelettes forestière*. This afternoon are the stocks: veal, Chinese chicken, *glace de viande*. It's a world without end. Back upstairs, I let her try a tartelette.

"Sweet Baby Jesus!" she says, would swoon, perhaps, were it not for the uniform, composure woven directly into its steely sheen.

"It's the truffles," I tell her.

She kisses me on the mouth, cries out, "You're a doll!" I should open a restaurant, she tells me, her arm waving across the food wondering what to choose next. Yes, I say, that would be fun, a restaurant, but there is the family, the wife, the son and the daughter, absent as they might be at the moment, and for the next several hours, I presume, far away from the bedroom, where the bed is, etc. etc.

"And there's the new laws," I say.

"Yes, there's those," she says between bites of *pommes*, "damned things. This is delicious."

"It's the kirsch," I tell her.

"There's a movement afoot," she says.

"A movement?" I say. "Afoot?"

"To repeal the laws."

"Really."

"Mm-hm."

"What if people don't want it?" I ask.

"Don't want it?"

"What if we're happy, all things considered, with the way things are?"

"The way things are?"

"Yes, the standing dish. And leery of any projected *boule-versements*."

"You can't be happy."

"As a pig in shit, some might say," I reply.

"That's not true," she says.

"No," I say, "you're right. It's not. Not at all."

For Sheila is still off somewhere, preparing the apparatuses, combing the swamps, harpooning the sea hogs, fish bats, wanderoos – something, anyway, that's kept her from carrying out the conjugal vows for nigh on three weeks, while this, this comely gasmaid talks of movements, practically throws herself at me and my *poularde chanteclair*. What's a boy to do? That could be my motto, the motto of thousands like me, the displaced *jefes grandes* of the recent past, sent home under the new laws.

The new laws. My friend Harley could go on forever discussing them. Harley stays at home, like me, discharged by an employer who was, after all, only abiding by the word of the people, but there is great bitterness in Harley's heart.

"Fuckers," I remember him saying.

The employer, he told me, had rolled into his office on his way to the pastry table. "Cash in your chips, Harley my boy!" the employer had said. "There's one too many of you on the books."

"One too many what?" Harley had asked. Harley's big on confrontation, will never learn, never learn.

"Pudgy cirrhotic number twiddlers. Pasty dyspeptic wampum shufflers." Words to that effect. "A superfluity has been declared, fellows like you are the sorry cause of an inequity, an inequity in need of repair. Time to act is now, say the legislators. So take it like a man, m'boy. Dime's waiting on the nickel."

"Fuckers," Harley said. He took it personally, couldn't swallow at all the sacrifice he was being asked to make, and now sits at home drinking contraband liquor smuggled by roving gangs of displaced militia men, six bucks a quart. He will go on about the new laws the way some will go on about the assassination of presidents, if you let him. I do not.

He sits in my living room now, tuned to the *Alfie Durant Show*, a glass of Seagram's in his fist, a plate of fresh *frivolités* in his lap. Today on *Alfie*, he yells to me in the kitchen, the panel of experts will discuss the Politics of Meat, Penile Implants, and Transgendered Hockey Coaches: Are They Tough Enough for the Big Leagues?

"Well, well, well," says Harley. "Don't get me wrong, if they can do the job, and all that, but what I object to . . ." and launches into another glum appraisal of the new laws, which I tune out with the blender set on crush for my Margarita.

Some time later, I enter with my drink. I must admit it's a little sad seeing Harley like this, a buzz on at three in the afternoon, bits of *frivolités* clinging to his copper beard, tabloid TV holding his bearish gaze. Harley's a big man, hairy-knuckled, malodorous, strong as a buffalo. The kind of man meant to trudge off to work every morning, utterly satisfied with the hatred of his job. The new laws are not perfect, no one has said they are.

"Meat," I say to Harley, diverting him from his favourite subject. "Politic or impolitic?"

Harley edges forward on the sofa. "Well, that depends on who you listen to," he says and swigs at his glass. "If you're with that pantywaist with the gummy hair and the grappling iron through his lower lip, you're against. If you're with that fellow with the cheese-grater haircut and the Teddy Roosevelt glasses – bets on whether his girlfriend is a sheep – you're for. Then you've got the namby-pamby dietitian, Christ, she's a piece of work, yammering on about your fatty acids, your protein deficiencies, your low-cal high-fibre what-nots, your respect for other people's gastronomic beliefs. Don't know what Alfie was thinking, I'd club her with a . . ."

"And the implants?" I ask.

"They had one guy on, telling how his went berserk."

"It's a peculiar world, Harley."

"You can bet your Peking duck on that, little buddy."

Yesterday, two things happened. First, in the city, a deer killed itself by jumping off the fourth floor of the Safeway Parking Tower. The deer had wandered through the entrance to the tower and strolled up the ramps to Level 400, and it was killed instantly, say the newspapers, when it stepped off the open ledge and fell fifty feet to the concrete sidewalk. I imagine the deer: its splayed legs stiffen with surprise in the air. Or perhaps it goes ass over tea kettle, its legs pointing heavenward, its black deer-lips parting with a final exhausted sigh.

This is the angle the papers take:

DEER MAKES SUICIDAL LEAP FROM SAFEWAY TOWER

I always imagined deer as having a pretty good time of it, except during hunting season, of course. Even then, the hunters are often so drunk they hunt cows instead, who are less fleet of foot, easier to track. So I wouldn't have been surprised if, say, Harley was the one hurling himself from the Safeway Tower. But a deer. That's a whole other story, one in which we allow for deer a quantity of consciousness and choice, in which we grant them a capacity for despair, if we believe the newspapers. No, a car scared it, and off it sailed. That must be what happened.

Which brings me to the second thing. Sheila came back, came and went. There was laundry in the chute, an army surplus bag crumpled next to the front closet, extra dishes in the sink, the asparagus frittata in the fridge was half eaten. I was out at the fishmonger's, the special was Arctic char. How often does that happen? There was a quad-ruled note drooping from the fridge door:

*Honey, sorry, had to run. Something happening back at the
lab. Someone set the subjects loose. Will call.*
Love, Sheila.

I took it as significant that she felt she had to sign her name.
Things, I decided, were moving increasingly beyond hope. That
was the correlative significance of the deer. The children –
teenagers, for God's sake – had started whining for their mother.
The empty Hennessy bottles were piling up. The dog had taken
to heaping dead cats in the yard.

So something's got to give. There are deer, Sheila, leaping
from tall buildings. There are things beyond science.

I told Harley about the gasmaid, and he was overjoyed to hear of
the movement to repeal the laws, running out to join up right
away. I fear Harley is not exactly what they're looking for, but
that's the nature of movements, isn't it, collecting on their
merry progress a variety of fringes, some more frayed, vocifer-
ous, lunatic than others. The bean curd people, for instance, are
a decent bunch on the whole, caring as they do for animals,
hawking their cheese-like wares, but there are those like my
deranged daughter, obsessed beyond belief, there are those who
go too far, abducting pigs, blowing up ranchers, setting crates of
frozen Christmas turkeys adrift at sea in a desperate vegetarian
protest. The movement for repeal may find such a person in
Harley, all too willing to blow things up, hunt things down, run
things through. He's born for the *Alfie Durant Show*, where our
more troubled citizens flaunt their tragedies, manias, and fleshy
abnormalities within the purview of their neighbours. He will
be there one day soon, happy to explain why so-and-so needed to
be tied to the back of a Dodge Caravan and shown what-for, and
if that means he's bound for the glory of the big house, then so
be it, good for the cause, etc., etc.

Meanwhile, I'm out walking the dog. He busies himself
sniffing at the well-spoored sidewalks, urinating freely about
the neighbourhood, knocking down small children, while I
rehearse speeches aimed at Sheila, who is still off somewhere,
rescuing the hop toads, roosterfish, wood ducks.

Sheila, I'll say, there is the world of science, that world in which you perform your variety of miracles, poking and cutting and spooning and measuring, all the things you're so good at and for which the government feeds you stupendous amounts of cash. Diseases will be cured, behavioural tics catalogued, whole stretches of the planet saved, because of your particular genius, perplexing as it might be to me. Who knows what you'll do next, what you do now, the world of science is such a mystery to most of us, the laymen, cheering the scientists on in their march to a better world. It all seems so heroic from a distance, a shining example of the shrewd new laws.

Then there is my world. It's a very rich one, full as it is of my own domestic miracles, the handsome house, the *gastronomie*, the survival of the children who, despite their profound troubles and mutilated bodies, are good as far as children go. It is made up of tiny, multifarious moments and random encounters, of shop owners, gasmaids, revolutionaries, lost children, distraught men. And it has not had you in it for too long.

That's what I'll say to her the moment I see her, the moment she calls. The world of science is not the be-all and end-all, I'll remind her. I salute you and your work, whatever it may be, but there is a bottle of burgundy on the table, there is a *selle d'agneau duchesse* in the oven, there is me, sitting, waiting, wondering, wanting.

SARAH WITHROW

Ollie

Ihate those weaselly weasels all over the place with their weasel looks and their weasel lines and their weaselly humpback hairdos with that weasel oil all combed in. They shouldn't be allowed to talk to each other on the subway like that, with their little ferret faces snapping at each other, their little noses crinkling and chops clacking with clickety high-pitched rodent squeals. I hate them. Just look at their tight pants, covering their fur – their legs must be sweating out all the dirt on their knees. They will sweat all down their legs and leave little weasel puddles when they get off of here. They should stop talking. I can't stand their talking. Squeak. Squeak. Chatchachachat-chat-rat-ta-chat. Machine gun. What's he looking at?

"Don't you look at me. What are you looking at? My pink shirt? My mother gave me this shirt – it's not for you to look at." He's still looking at me. What makes him special? My mother gave me this shirt. She washed it last week at the laundromat even when vagrants were there. I told her it was too pink. It looks like the inside of a sinus. "I bet your mother never bought you anything. Don't you look at me. Shut your eyes." Look at those weasels looking at me. Freaks. I bare my teeth at you. "Hhhhssssssss. Weasels. Good. You should be scared." Here's where I get off. Thank God, I don't have to look at those weasels any more.

They always move too slowly on the subway platform. "Excuse me. Excuse me. Excuse me. Excuse me. Excuse me.

Excuse me." You'd think with a shirt like this that sticks out they would see me coming with those eyes they have in the back of their heads. Everyone has too much hair. "I've got to go to the hardware store before it closes. Excuse me. Excuse me." They should all leave me alone. Can't they see I'm wearing this siren of a shirt? "Woooowooooowooooowooooowooooowooooowoooo." Now they're moving.

It's beautiful out. I can breathe. Ollie's made it off the subway and safely out. I wonder if she wants to go to the hardware store. No. That's enough. I'll go – this is my neighbourhood. There's Tanya with her baby. "Hi, Tanya. Hi, Ruthie. Isn't she getting so big? Every time I see her she's got more hair."

"Really? I guess I'm with her all the time so I don't really notice it." Tanya looks a little tense. We talk about her husband Greg going on a business trip for a week and her feeling pent up in their apartment. She thinks she's reverting. She found herself sucking on the baby's pacifier the other day and liking it. I told her it's got to be better than living with my mother.

"I found myself acting like a cranky old bitch the other day and liking it." Ha ha. Toodledoo, and off I go. She doesn't know the half of it. I love being Ollie. I love the way Ollie really gives it to them. Ollie doesn't take shit from anyone. Here's what Ollie would say to Greg: "You're going away with all them penis-brains to come up with some penisbrain ideas for selling penis-brain-type cars? Your baby could die and you'd be in some penisbrain hotel boardroom comparing suits, chewing on your ballpoint pens and drinking coffee with real cream poured from tax deductible crystal. Your baby could die while you're gone. But the future of the world depends on your penisbrain conference. Who's going to take care of me? What do you think they invented phones for – you've got seven of them."

Light bulbs. We can't have the ones from the supermarket. We have to have the ones from the hardware store. Mom says they last longer and she checks the bags to make sure I get them at the right place. I have twice gotten away with using an old hardware store bag to hide supermarket-bought light bulbs. But that takes planning.

I discovered Ollie in the bathroom mirror about two years

ago. I had the water running to drown out Mom's hollering for tea, with lemon and honey and it better be Orange Pekoe and it better be the round bags – as if I'd dare buy any other kind. I looked in the mirror and there she was. My eyebrows have always looked a little cross since I over-plucked them when I was fifteen. I can enhance the effect by furrowing them. My whole face changes when I'm Ollie. My whole body changes. My shoulders ride up close to my ears and I can feel the veins tense in my neck and arms. Ollie's always got her fists clenched, ready to fight. She spit at the mirror when she saw herself. She put her mousey hair in a tight ponytail and tightened it more. She put her lower teeth in front of her upper teeth. Gnash. Gnash. Her thin lips accentuated the effect. She hit her sides with her clenched fists. She pursed her lips and hyperventilated through them, holding her fists against her ears. Shut up. Shut up.

"Did you get the light bulbs? I hope you went to the hardware store. I'm making lasagna, but it's not going to have any meat in it because that stuff you brought back yesterday was too fatty."

I put the bags on the counter and check the oven. "Oh really? I got the lean stuff like you said."

"Get your nose out of there, girlie. You trying to heat the whole neighbourhood? You didn't get it from the butcher's, you got it from the supermarket. I don't like not knowing who handles my beef."

We've been through this argument a thousand times. I say it's easier for me to go to the supermarket, but she says she doesn't trust them. They're just in it for the money. Like everybody isn't. She doesn't like me patronizing stores where the owner doesn't work behind the counter. Then she says that she could do the shopping if I can't do it right and I imagine her falling on Parliament and breaking a hip and telling the ambulance drivers that, yes, she has a daughter who lives with her but she has to do all the shopping. And that's the end of the argument. I'm going to hear about this meat all night now.

"Tastes good even without the beef in it. It's a good thing you have a talented mother."

I have lately taken to grinding up Nytol in her after-dinner tea. I know it's not very kind of me, especially since I'm often Ollie when I'm doing it: taking the pills from my purse (where she won't find them) and crushing them under a teaspoon, pretending they are arsenic. I just couldn't stand listening to her go on about not being able to sleep and refusing to take the stuff herself because she claims it's unnatural and gives her indigestion. Now she's in bed by ten and sound, sound asleep by ten-thirty.

That's when I bring out the wine and turn on my Spanish music and dance with Ollie in me all over the first floor. I shake my hands in the air until the air feels thick and liquid around them. I spaz dance, rolling my head around and convulsing my body to propel it forward through the living room. I tear the crocheted doilies from the useless little table tops and shake them in the air. I am a mad flamenco dancer, a fevered gypsy queen, and my fortune is my ability to dance this dance with my eyes closed without ever disturbing the furniture. The Spanishness infects me all the way from my gypsy feet through to my lashing gypsy tongue which trills as I round the kitchen corner and again down the hall back to the living room. Twirling, swirling, and shaking with craziness is this dance of the sleeping mother.

I hide the wine in the back of the toilet. I am thirty-four years old and haven't had a lover in seven years. It's clear I need a vacation.

On Saturdays I go to the pharmacy to pick up Mom's heart medicine. She's on my health plan as my designated dependant. My company is very progressive. I would even be allowed to get my birth control pills covered if I was taking them. I try not to be bitter, but it is difficult watching all my friends fall in love and get married when nothing is happening in my life. I know it's not Mom's fault – except that it partially is. I just don't like the men that like me. If they smile they remind me of toothpaste salesmen at dentists' conventions. If they nod they remind me of jack-in-the-boxes. If they converse they remind me of Oprah. If they take my hand they remind me of soap opera heroes. They don't seem real. And the ones I like haven't met me yet.

I have to go to the pharmacy on the corner of Parliament and

Carlton and I can't cheat because they put fucking labels on the containers. Another reason I like supermarket shopping is because I can bring Ollie out with me. They know me at all of the stores Mom has me go to. It always feels like a violation to me when they call me by my first name. Thanks, Maria. The sun's sure shining today, Maria. How's your Mom doing, Maria? Can I get you anything else, Maria? It seems like they say it to prove they know it. Mom likes that they do this. She likes to be told "The Butcher says Hi." She gets this smug, happy wee grin on her face that screams "See?" But they don't know me at all. All they know is two pounds of beef and a quarter-kilogram Havarti and heart pills for a month and caraway rye sliced. And they use my name like it's a demographic label. But I'm me. And I'm Ollie and nobody knows me whole enough to say my name properly.

Look at this wiseguy hogging the Pharmacist's time. Who cares about the pain in his leg. Who cares if his wife is visiting relatives in Florence. I've been here for seven minutes now and I'm through looking at the backs of all the vitamin jars. My transactions never take more than forty seconds. Move it, lard-ass, there's work to be done. He's so pathetic. He can't even take being lonely for a week without taking it out on the local shop-keepers. "Blah, blah, blah, blah. Are you going to take all day? Leave, already. I don't have time to listen to your lardass life story." This is the first time Ollie has come out without me wanting her to. I've stunned him into submission and he backs away. I can feel my face flushing. I bring my hand up to my mouth and sock myself with the fist that it is. Oh no. The man gathers up his things and leaves the store. I wait a few seconds before moving up to the wicket – maybe he'll think it was some-one else. But there's nobody else here.

Over the wicket I can see the Pharmacist's back in a crouch. When he comes up he takes one look at me and bursts out laughing.

"Maria! I'm sorry. I'm sorry. Lardass? You really showed him, boy."

"I really didn't mean to be rude," I tell him in my softest voice, but he is having none of it.

"I wish you had come in half an hour ago. I had to listen to

Mrs. Picklous's daughter's wedding stories. Maybe I'll set up a chair for you right here – you can be my official bore harasser."

"I'm so embarrassed." I feel like crying. But under the shame I feel Ollie's adrenalin coursing through my veins. I fall back against the vitamin counter and pull over a perfume carousel trying to maintain my balance. I'm on the floor surrounded by vitamin C and something called *Fleurs de Ma Vie*. He brings me behind the counter, sits me on a chair and gets me a glass of water. It is the first time I have ever seen his legs. He is wearing shorts and sandals under his white smock. This is most unexpected. I cannot help feeling my cheeks with the back of my hand. He is still chuckling and muttering "Lardass" under his breath.

"Here you go," he says, handing me the water.

"Thanks. Really, I'm so sorry."

"Relax – everybody snaps sometimes. Actually, in this neighbourhood, I'm surprised it doesn't happen more often. At least you didn't break anything." I don't know what to say so I just drink the water, looking straight into the cup as I'm doing it to avoid eye contact. My hand is shaking. I can see through the glass that he has his hands on his hips. I wish he wouldn't hover like that. He leans over and takes the glass and puts it on the counter. "Come on," he says, taking my hand. "I want to show you something." He leads me to the back of the store. His hand is clean and warm – not sticky. My wrist is blushing. We reach a stack of boxes piled up six high. He passes them to me as he takes them down. The wall behind has a large hole in it. He takes the boxes from me and puts them on the floor. He takes my hand and moulds it into a fist again and rams it through the hole in the wall. "BAM. That's how that got there. I broke two fingers. Now that's stupid. Know why I did that? I'm not a violent guy, you know. That's there because a shipment was late. That's there because I had a bad day. I never laid a finger on anybody – not for cheating me, not for stealing from me, not for screwing me around. But a shipment is late and WHAMMO."

I can't help thinking that he had laid a finger on me. A few of them in fact.

"How do you solve a problem like Maria?" My mother sings the song lowly. This *Sound of Music* tune is the only song she knows with my name in it – she claims. I have to hear her hum or sing it every day. It makes me want to stuff socks down her throat and duct tape her lips together. Sometimes it makes me want to throw up, and once I did. She asks me whether I've remembered that next week is Canada Day. She actually asks me if I have a date to go the fireworks. Like that even happens any more. And then she says, "Well, I hope you're going. You really should get out more." It's all I can do to prevent Ollie from telling her "look who's talking, you friendless, useless, draining old cretin." Then, as if she's read my mind, she tells me that she's going to go visit my aunt in a couple of weeks and then she tells me that the woman she sits next to in church has invited her over for dinner next Friday and would that be okay with me.

"Fine," I say and wander out of the kitchen, which is really her domain despite the fact that I've bought everything in it. When I am safely in my room, Ollie rips one of my pillowcases apart – first down the seams and then in strips. I braid the strips in groups of three and then unbraid them and think about making a rag rug in my spare time. I look in the mirror and I've got little threads all in my hair and stuck to my black sweater where Mom will notice them for sure. I am a rag rug. Now.

Once I was a rug rat ruling the back alley. Once I was a champion, a hero, a winner. I was the sneakiest Kick the Can player that ever was. I was hailed by the neighbourhood children. They begged for me to help them, pleading with their eyes, stretching their arms, as far as they dared, outside the chalk-drawn prisons, reaching for me with dirty fingernails, calling for me all the summer day long until the twilight ate their lips and mothers appeared on back porches to wave them in for macaroni dinners.

I was the brave and taller than the rest, my well-bruised legs stretching nearly three feet beyond the bottoms of my short nylon shorts. I became the brave because I was too big to hide. I made no attempt to burrow into the deepest recesses of Mr. Harper's junk-filled garage, or slink behind the corn growing in the Kempvilles' garden. Too predictable. I never peed *my* pants because I was afraid to get caught. I was the stealthiest of the spies, lurking carefully – and generally in the open – but out of view of the It. Behind It. Astride It. I studied It and I knew where It would move next, where It would look next. Where It thought I might be, for the secret of where I was presented Its greatest challenge. I was Its greatest foe. Any unguarded moment could result in my Kicking the Can, setting free Its prisoners and send-ing them scurrying down the alley to the triumphant sound of my top-lunged victory scream: "Ollie-Ollie-Oxen-Free."

It's kind of pathetic that I think of those as my glory days. Still, looking in the mirror I think how nice it would be to have my eyebrows back. I crunch them up for a minute muttering, "Ollie, Ollie, Ollie, Ollie, Ollie."

Huge walking peanut-ridden turds. Tourist turds, weebling snail-slow in front of Ollie, asking for it. Wall of weebley white-panted turdstras stepping to look in every stupid window like they've never seen a mall before. Like malls aren't all they ever see. Licking their turdish ice cream waffle cones full to the brim with calories galore. I'll push your faces into them. I'll smear them up and down your white turd-infested clothes.

They stop in front of a luggage store – like, how did they get this far without it? – and Ollie can't take it any more. I barge through them, banging their bums with my shopping bags and screaming: "I am soooooooooooooo sorry. Soooooooooo sooooo sorry." Because I am in the Eaton Centre the supply of turds is endless. I spot another group of them just up ahead by the foun-tain and march towards them, bending down and readjusting my bags to secure them for the event. I plunge forward, knocking a kiddy turd off balance, but I said I was "Soooorrrry. I am sooo, sooo, sorry." The turds are cursing me in loud American voices. But I've apologized. More weebles at two o'clock. I prepare to launch another assault, when down from somewhere falls a familiar name.

"Maria, Maria . . ." and a whistle. I look up. Waving, all smiles from the top of the escalator, is the Pharmacist. The turds I just levelled are catching up to me as he shoves his way down the escalator. I am stunned still, only my neck moves looking both ways at the world closing in on me. The weebles reach me first and the Father turd yells in my face but I can't hear him. Then the Pharmacist is by my side holding my arm and poking the Father turd in the chest and dragging me away, up the escalator and outside to a bench. He sits me down and covers his face with his hands. When he lowers them his face is open in pleasured shock.

"Wham. Bam. Thank you Ma'am. . . . That was a day's entertainment."

Because he is amused and because Mom's out of town, I invite him for dinner. He brings me a bunch of irises "from Rula's place" and I know where he's talking about because Mom makes me get produce there. I picture him telling an inquiring Rula where he's going for dinner. Braggart. Just because he runs his own business he thinks he's part of the neighbourhood elite. He keeps calling the neighbourhood Cabbagetown and I say that most Saturdays it's a fight between the drunks and the yuppies for sidewalk space. He says that yuppies take up less space even with strollers because at least they move whereas the drunks monopolize their spots for a good part of the day.

"Why are you pretending it's a good neighbourhood?" Ollie asks. "It's not Rosedale. You aren't like, Pharmacist to the stars."

But he has witnessed her harsher moments and is obviously here because he enjoys a challenge. "I never said it was a good neighbourhood. I think it's a good thing it's a bad neighbourhood. I think the yuppies come to see the drunks."

His smile is inappropriate. He should not toy with Ollie. She bites.

I've served spaghetti, which automatically goes with wine. I am forced at one point to retrieve the bottle from the toilet tank. In the mirror, I watch myself remove the lid to the toilet tank, remove the bottle, and replace the lid. I know how to do it without making noise now. I wish I knew how to do it without looking in the mirror. We drink too much. I put on my Spanish music and he joins me in my dance, donning a doily for the finale. He leers at me through the holes in the lace. He eats me with his eyes.

What do I know about him after all? Only that he enjoys the way Ollie's edges grate on him, like the satisfying scratch of pieces of wall digging into a fist going through it. He is calling to Ollie with his evil eyes. It's her he wants.

"Get away, get away, get away from me." I shoo him down the hall back to the living room then run past him up the stairs.

"Maria?"

I run into the washroom and lock the door. I spend far too much time in here. The mirror echoes the fear on my face. It is wrong for me to be scared.

"You're getting more wine, right?" he asks. He knows too much. He thinks he can know me.

"Wrongo. You're wrong," Ollie yells in her razor-blade voice. Everything is wrong because I want him to say my name again. I squeeze myself into the spot between the toilet and the bathtub and ache for him to say my whole name again. "Please," I invoke the power of the magic word and wonder what it will do for me. I can hear his hand stroking the door as he explores further his relationship with walls.

"I swear to God, Maria. I don't know what's wrong, but we can't figure it out like this."

I don't know either. I'm too tired to know. I don't even know how I got here. I don't even know who I am here. My brain is numb and my fists are rubbing my ugly, ugly eyebrows that will never grow back. As long as I live. Forever. I am doomed to go through life with a practically bald forehead. Can't he see what's written all over my face? Emotional illiterate. Pimple-cream-pushing-tightass-drunk-gawking-yuppie-lover. Germ. Pill.

"I'm going to kick this door in. Maria? I'm not going to let you do this. I'm going to count to ten and I'm going to kick it in." He starts his count, measuring perfectly the beats between the numbers. Calm, cool, collected, and brave to want her so much to do this.

I stretch my hands out, palms open, fingers straining in reach, and I listen, for the victorious sound of the one swift kick.

KRISTEN DEN HARTOG

Wave

The second time her father leaves Hannah is the same height as the blue pine tree in the front yard. A boating accident. He got caught in the propeller, like seaweed, so parts of him were chopped off, bleeding. Hannah hasn't been told directly but she knows.

To the funeral she wears a yellow sun dress with straps that tie over each shoulder and also the hood from her snowsuit, the string pulled tight in a triple knot under her chin. Vivian says this is ridiculous, to wear an unzipped snowsuit hood in July, especially to a funeral. She tries to tug it loose but Hannah hangs on. Holds the hood close around her face and screeches. Vivian yanks the hood, gets a fistful of Hannah's hair, and even though Hannah feels the hairs coming right out of her head, she keeps screeching and hanging on. Vivian lets go, shoves Hannah out the front door and into the driveway, where Uncle Tim waits in the car, adjusting the rearview. Hannah's head throbs. Each hair hole stings. She rubs the hood against her scalp.

Too, Hannah's mother wears a hat – black and wide-brimmed – and makes no comment. She rides between them in the back seat of Uncle Tim's convertible, one hand holding her hat in place, the other squeezing a wad of Kleenex. Her dress is short, tight, and she sits with her feet on the hump, bony knees close together, the freckles there fading into her tan.

It is hot inside the snowsuit hood and hard to see out the window. Hannah's head moves but the hood won't so she peers partly outside and partly at the crisp red lining. On Birch Street children skipping rope stop and point, half laughing, as Uncle Tim's Rambler rolls by. Hannah knows why. Knows too the half-laugh feeling. Last year Angel Sinclair's mom died and Hannah felt the giggles bubbling inside, lips twitching, because it was thrilling somehow. Exciting to know about Mrs. Sinclair, who went so bald she lost even her lashes and eyebrows.

Hannah wears the hood for one week straight. *You'll get cooties*, Vivian says, *if you don't wash your hair*. Some of the kids at school have cooties – bus kids mostly, who live on the outskirts. Cooties jump from head to head so it's best not to sit next to a bus person in class or even hang your coat too close. Hannah's head itches thinking of cooties. She likes being in the hood though. Likes that things are muffled and far away. Uncle Tim scratches her head a lot now that she's in the hood. His finger-nails against the nylon bug her. Uncle Tim's nails are too long for a man, moons of dirt underneath. Hannah doesn't like him touching her, not even with the hood between them. His toe-nails are long too – yellow and curled down at the ends, like ugly hats for his toes. And hairs sprout from the skin there – black and wiry, like the hairs on arms and legs. Hannah doesn't know if her father's toes were sliced off in the accident or not. In life his toes were long and slender, the nails clean, flat and wide. She can picture these. His straggly red beard. Blue swimming-pool eyes. Bony nose. But she can't see them all at once. He comes to her in pieces. There are bits of him, maybe, floating in the river.

A bright day. Hannah squints in the sun, head pressed into the screen, pushing it out, making it lumpier, looser, which would anger her mother but Hannah doesn't care, keeps pushing, watching, listening for her father's Alfa Romeo to buzz around the corner, too fast, he always drives too fast, and on the high-way he lets you roll the windows down, front and back, and get all blown around even if you're eating ice cream and your hair gets sticky. Hannah watches the street. Speeding around the cor-ner any second now, so fast there might be skid marks when he stops, and he leaves the keys in because who wants to steal this old heap anyway. He gets out, stands in the street and waves,

hair sticking up in front where his cowlick is, like Hannah's, and
Hannah waves back and pushes the door open and hollers across
the lawn even though she just saw him yesterday and the day
before and the day before that. Hannah listens. Any time now,
just to say hi and pick up the mail and there's always a stack of
it for him, sometimes with his name spelled funny because people are always getting names wrong that don't come from
England or Scotland and then *Gotta go!* and Hannah hops on his
back and flops out to the car and then slides off him and waves
and waves and waves until he's right around the corner and out
of sight and he waves all that time too, looking in his rearview
and not even watching where he's going, that's how great a driver he is. Hannah waits. Presses hard into the screen. The pattern of it now embedded in her forehead.

Uncle Tim lives on the outskirts, with the bus people, where
the grass is so patchy and dry you don't even need to mow it. To
get to his house you have to drive out on the highway, past the
population sign, which faces the other way, and turn right on a
gravel road with no name. His house is little and lopsided.
Under the couch and even beside his bed are dirty dishes, sometimes puffy green with mould, and Hannah's mother gathers
them up, shaking her head and giggling. Uncle Tim shrugs and
says, *What can I say, I'm a bachelor.* Hannah wanders through
the house, trying not to touch things. She thinks if there were
cooties anywhere, there would be cooties here. Uncle Tim's
bedroom smells musty and sour, like unwashed sheets. Short
black hairs scatter his bathroom sink. Nose hairs? Ear hairs? In
life Hannah's father's hair was strawberry blond, like Hannah's
and Vivian's and even Hannah's mother's – the four of them
wearing hats in summer to keep their part-lines from burning.
Hannah thinks it's silly calling Uncle Tim Uncle Tim, pretending he fits in. He's too big, she thinks. Too dark to be one
of them.

Uncle Tim is not the first and Vivian says he won't be the last.
Uncle Tim is the first uncle though. The first to make himself
related. Hannah thinks of Mr. Unwin, who came between her
father and Uncle Tim. Lived with his mother so couldn't sleep

over. Hannah and Vivian called him Mr. Onion, plugged their
noses when he came around. Mr. Onion was jittery, almost bald.
Wore socks inside his sandals. He loaned Hannah's mother a
stereo and when Hannah's mother dumped him she put the
stereo outside on the step, a note stuck to it, flapping in the
breeze. Hannah's mother and Hannah and Vivian had to duck
behind the couch when Mr. Onion arrived but Hannah could see
him from her hiding place, struggling with the stereo and two
big speakers. She could see the note, too, standing up in the
wind, stamped at the bottom with her mother's lipstick.
Watched him lug the stereo all the way to his car, then turn
around to bring it back. Now Hannah's mother plays Uncle
Tim's records on it, twangy country tunes about cheating and
falling to pieces.

Today they stay forever at Uncle Tim's. Vivian reads outside
in the hammock, swatting black flies and flicking their
squashed bodies from her bare pink legs. She's too heavy for the
hammock. Her bum a big round melon stretching the twine
apart. Hannah wishes she could make the twine unravel just by
staring at it, see Vivian drop in the dirt. The hammock's the only
good thing about Uncle Tim's place and Vivian hogs it.

Inside, Hannah's mother and Uncle Tim lie at opposite ends
of the couch, feet touching. All day the fan blows on them as they
giggle and whisper. It's boring at Uncle Tim's. Only six houses on
his no-name road and the kids who live in them are bus kids.

By the time her mother is ready to leave it's almost dark. The
sky hangs navy blue, the air cool and damp on Hannah's skin.
Hannah stretches out on the back seat, head against one door,
feet flat on the other. She still fits in this space, but barely.
Vivian climbs into the front seat, rests her dirty feet on the
dash. Outside, Uncle Tim's arm circles Hannah's mother's waist
and pulls her in. Hannah stares up at them. They look funny
upside down. Cartoons whose eyes and noses and mouths got
drawn on after the rest of them was made. Uncle Tim kisses
Hannah's mother long and sloppy on the mouth, then gives
quick pecks to her nose and forehead, and Hannah's mother's
hand touches his sweaty face, not something you'd touch if you
didn't have to.

Wave to Uncle Tim, Hannah's mother tells them as she moves the car down the lane. Hannah ignores her. Listens to the crickets, the tires rolling on the gravel. Watches Vivian's hand slip out the side window, held high and still in a false wave. On the highway Hannah's mother switches on the radio and hums along off-key, fingernails clicking against the steering wheel. Hannah stares at the tiny holes in the ceiling. With a pen she could connect the dots. The ceiling is like a big insole for a shoe. Soft and cushy. If the car rolled it might protect them, their three pale heads stuffed against it.

Sunrise. Sky brightens behind the curtains. Hannah lies in bed, the sheet pulled up to her nose. Inhales. Sucks cotton into her nostrils. If she concentrates she can open the curtains without ever touching them. Without moving from the bed. Hannah holds her breath, flexes all her muscles until her head tingles and orange spots blur her vision. Once she moved her dresser this way. Just a smidge, but she can do it again if she tries hard enough. Her father says anything is possible. Hannah presses two fingers to each temple. If she had been there she could have stopped it. Used her powers and zeroed in on her dad spraying to pieces in the water. She closes her eyes. Sees it before it happens. Squints, concentrates. And her dad springs from the water in maroon swimming trunks with white stripes, spins through the air like a baseball, lands beside her on the beach, wet, laughing.

If she had been there she could have stopped it. Anything's possible. Should have gone afterwards, even, when Chief Bartley came to the door and she knew right away something was wrong. Should have gone because you never know, it might not have been too late. Her mother bending down, freckled knees cracking, and Hannah can feel the something-wrong feeling, like when he left the first time. Her skin hot blotches, head twitching. Stomach fluttery, light, then heavy and rolling, like she has to poo. Hannah's mother holding the ends of Hannah's braids – *something awful* – and Hannah runs, screen door banging, feet burning on the pavement all the way to the beach, big strides, knees high, arms working. She can see him on the sand, parts missing, flooding blood, and if she concentrates she can locate the pieces, gather them up with her mind muscles and stick them back on him, mop up the wounds.

The first time her father leaves, though her mother says she couldn't possibly remember, Hannah sees him from the back, walking down the hall with his shoes on, a no-no, hard grey suitcase in his hand. Hannah's mother says no, you were at a sleepover. And too, we didn't have the carpet then. Hannah stands at the hall's end, watching, Dad smaller and smaller, not turning to wave. Into the kitchen and around the corner and she hears the door open, then close, and the Alfa start up, muffler dragging on the driveway, tied on but falling off. Stands still till she can't hear any more and then in her room cries and cries into her bedspread so hard and so long there are sore creases on her face when she gets up, and later she tells people, no, he didn't really leave, not like that, he was too tall for this house so he had to move away where the ceilings were higher but still he comes to visit every day, so really it's just like normal. And at school the teacher smooths wide pieces of pale grey paper on their desks and says, *Draw your house*, and Hannah draws on both sides, her own green house with red doors and the pine tree, chives poking up out of a pot by the side door, and then the place her father lives, a big apartment building downtown with polka dots of every colour.

Hannah's in the bath, sloshing in warm water, bubbles up to her neck. Her mother sits on the tub's edge in a shortie nightgown, stuffs cotton balls between her toes and paints the nails cherry red. *What do you think?* she says. *You'd get to ride the school bus every day.* Hannah thinks of cooties, combs her fingers through her hair. Vivian leans in the doorway, arms crossed. No way would she share a room. They'd have to build an extension, she says, so she could have her own space. Hannah scoops bubbles. Pictures Uncle Tim's square-box house with a piece added on. Hannah a bus kid. Stretched socks sagging around her ankles. Cooties and moths gnawing tiny holes in her T-shirts. In the mornings before she brushed she'd have to splash water around the sink to wash the nose hairs down. And black Uncle Tim hairs might wind up woven into her sweaters just from being around him so much. Hannah dunks a face cloth in the bath, sucks water from it. *No*, she tells her mother. Hannah's mother half-smiles, wipes polish from a flap of toe-skin. *What if he came here?* says Hannah's mother. *No way*, says Vivian. Hannah shakes her head, slow, firm. *No way*. Hannah's mother fake-laughs, cheeks pink beneath her freckles. *Okay*, she says. Shrugs.

The house is messy. Little piles of Hannah's father's things on the couch and the dining room table. Hannah presses her hand into a pillowy stack of shirts – navy blue, baby blue, royal blue, sky blue, robin's egg blue, swimming-pool blue. Everything of his is here now, back where it started. Only rolling dust balls left in the apartment downtown – clumps made from his hair and belly-button lint and the tiniest flakes of his skin. Hannah smells the shirts but his smell is gone already. Hannah's mother has washed the clothes. What fits will go to Uncle Tim, she says. He could use a few things. Hannah shudders. Uncle Tim's sweaty skin staining the collars, the underarms. Tufts of his back hair sprouting from her father's T-shirts.

Even the Alfa is here, oil splotching the garage floor. Hannah sits in the driver's seat, stretches to reach the pedals. Closes her eyes. Winter and her mother's car won't start, so here he comes, saves the day, and the four of them pile into the Alfa to drive downtown and in the parking lot Hannah leans forward between the two seats and says, *Kiss! Kiss good-bye!* and she sees their faces from the side, half-smiling. *Hannah!* her mother says, but her father tilts his head, kisses her mother's cheek with Hannah's face right close to theirs, and Hannah says, *On the mouth!* Hannah's mother laughs and her father laughs too and even though it's just a quick kiss, a peck where the lips stay closed and the tongues don't touch, Hannah's sure it's the start of something, something starting all over again.

Hannah opens her eyes. She can see just her cowlick in the rearview, tiny baby hairs that don't grow, dipping down on her forehead. Sometimes, from the side, Hannah can see Uncle Tim's tongue rolling in her mother's mouth.

Uncle Tim begins appearing in her father's shirts and staying over. Hannah's mother doesn't ask any more if it's okay. Sometimes he comes for dinner and that changes things. He says dinner isn't soup and a sandwich or even a bowl of noodles with Cheez Whiz. Hannah's mother prepares Shake 'n' Bake chicken, boiled potatoes, and canned peas, lays them on the plates in three sections so that nothing touches, but the pea water leaks, spreads, inches over.

They begin to eat a lot of meat. Uncle Tim brings his barbecue and sets it up in the back yard. Wears an apron splotched with grease from steaks and burgers. Hannah doesn't like the meat. Doesn't want to eat someone's leg or wing, chew on a rib. When he's finished his own, Uncle Tim grabs the bones from all their plates and gnaws the remnants. *What a waste*, he says, mouth greasy.

Late at night Hannah can hear them moan and murmur. She sneaks to the bathroom for cotton balls, stuffs them in her ears, but the balls fall out and she hears them again. She lies on her side, hands pressed against her ears, and that works for a while, but when she starts to sleep her hands slide off and she hears them again. She puts the cotton balls back in, ties her snowsuit hood tight around her head. If she thinks of something else, she can barely hear anything.

In the morning Uncle Tim's still there, a sour smell all around him, hair crushed on one side, sticking out on the other. His pyjamas are her father's, white with blue stripes. Dingier now, stretched at the knees and elbows.

On Labour Day weekend a man comes and asks for Darlene. Hannah's mother appears in her pink kimono. Squeals and pushes Hannah aside, hugs the man. The man's pants ride up at the ankles when he wraps his arms around Hannah's mother and Hannah looks at his socks, pale yellow with designs where the bone juts out. His hair is smoothed back with something greasy and it shines blue-black in the sunlight. Hannah's mother makes Harvey Wallbangers and sits outside with the man, laughing, her hair hanging over the back of her lawn chair.

That was Darrell, her mother says later, beaming. Hannah thinks of her mother's high-school dictionary, red, loose at the binding. On the inside cover it says D & D in big, loopy letters. Darrell & Darlene. Darlene & Darrell. Dare & Darl 4-ever 2-gether.

Darrell comes back the next day and takes them all to the parade in a white sports car that smells new and leathery inside. Hannah's mother wears a shortie tight T-shirt, a crescent moon of sweat beneath each boob. Dare buys them candy floss, pink for Vivian, blue for Hannah, and Hannah's mother says, *Oh no, Dare, I couldn't possibly. I'm not the girl I used to be.* She rests her hands lightly on her belly, pretending she's fat. Dare laughs a low ha ha ha laugh, whispers something Hannah can't hear. He lays his hand at Hannah's mother's rib cage, too close.

That night Dare stays over and Hannah stuffs the cotton balls in, ties the hood around her head.

Hannah wonders if now Uncle Tim will stop calling and coming around. She thinks of him out there, sweating in her father's clothes. She'd like to get the clothes back – with her mind muscles, maybe, but then Dare might end up in them. Dare is bigger than Uncle Tim. Even his own clothes pull apart between the buttons.

Sometimes Dare comes over and cooks shish kebabs on Uncle Tim's barbecue. Stabs pieces of onion and green pepper and mushroom, floppy cubes of pink meat. He teaches Hannah. *Make a pattern*, he says, showing her. She watches his mouth, lips thick but pale. The same colour as his skin. Hannah has seen her mother kiss the lips, stain them with her lipstick.

They eat outside at the picnic table because Dare says they should enjoy the warm weather while they can. Already the maples are past the bright-red stage. Hannah slides the pieces from her skewer, pushes the meat aside, now brownish-grey. No bone, so she doesn't know what part of the body this is, what animal it's from. She thinks of the pieces of her father that didn't go underground. The fish feeding on him. Chewing on a finger or a toe.

Hannah lies in bed and waits for Dare to go away. Thinks of her father's pull-out couch, blue plaid, now for sale at the Sally Ann where someone grubby will buy it. A bus kid sleeping on it. Maybe two bus kids, bringing in toe jam and cookie crumbs and pebbles from outside. Hannah slept there with Vivian warm beside her. Dad snoring in the other room. Deep breaths, in and out, rattly but steady, nice to hear. And then in the morning fried eggs with soft centres, toast cut in fingers for dipping. Coffee too, a treat. Half coffee, half milk, heaping spoons of brown sugar stirred in, blowing and sipping from blue plastic tube glasses. And then into the Alfa, all the windows down, weaving through town over the speed limit, taking the long way, up to the highway, past the population sign, and back again.

MARK ANTHONY JARMAN

Righteous Speedboat

For no animal admires another animal.

– Blaise Pascal

Even now the vibrating screen maims the very molecules of my eyes but I have to gaze. How many bent berserkers, how many peckerwood imposters will they call to the silver microphone before they call to me, here with my nigh-on ruined vision? No finish at the net and hands of stone, but I can read a play, backcheck like a madman, and I move malevolently inside a snarling wind. Pins go down. That ought to be worth *something*, a few paydays, a winning smile from the bank teller. Tampa could take me down there with their palmetto bugs. Need be I'll go to the moon, I'll skate on Mars.

Maybe a scrounging team will grab me in a late round. Scrounging is okay, late round is okay. I could help a club in the Colonial League, work my way up. Just give me a contract. Or else I'm toast. I'm over-age, I can't go back to my junior team. I burnt a few bridges there, pissed off the scunt-eyed coach. I caught an elbow in the nose and saw visions of gasping lightning while the guy with said elbow slid away like a pulse to score the winning goal, to bury it top-shelf. All season who had the best plus-minus on the club? *Moi.* I repeat: I had the best plus-minus on the team. Yet in front of everyone the coach really reamed me out. Up and down, went to town. He had no need to do that, to humiliate me.

Elbowed nose still throbbing, I moved in close to the coach, paused to get him wondering, feinted, then I gave his nose a shot: I clocked the coach. Nothing really. They want you to hit everyone else: *Him*, they say in Spokane, and you know what they mean. Bing bang bong. Do it to *them*, though, touch *them* and it's the end of the fucking world. They tell the reporters you're "difficult," you're a cancer on the team. Control freak wimps. Blue-legged fops. Pukely ticket-punchers. I say this much is obvious: the "difficult" players are the real action, living it, lean as whippets; they throb, eat at the air like engines.

I call my agent long-distance and he allows, *This is he*.

Doesn't look good, he says. Our noisy years are moments, he says.

I call my mother and she sighs, You had so much potential.

I'd call my friend from Salmon Arm but Ryan's lost his head. The bloody trail across the gravel road I still dream of, and the green radiator water burning my hair. Ryan's head rolling.

Once upon a time this was a happening bar but now it's a loser bar. The bar has no view at all, a pocked pallid concrete bunker, which is good. Night for day, no trees and no sky. You pay extra for trees and sky, the darkening harbour. You need no view. You need to hear your name echoing in that distant subsidized convention centre; those two sweet words in that room of tasteful blurred suits. Your name.

I like loser bars. They're quiet and I can think.

I think there is always some injustice. We depend on tales of injustice. At the small curved bar an intense young man is telling a dark-eyed woman his specific story of injustice. He's well-dressed: black custom-cut pants and a beautiful shirt that is white and tapered. Gel gleams evenly in his hair. I decide his name is Laszlo. Someone looks after Laszlo's cuticles. Laszlo smokes. He collects things: plenitude, kudos, ivory elephants. The young woman is listening yet she is clearly fidgety, restless. Her dark eyes move in a sad poised face. I watch her dark eyes shiver. Her lipstick is almost black. She shows her teeth in a sad brief smile and it is everything. You learn everything. I can't stand the idea that it's all random.

Here's a guy, Laszlo says, leaning right at her, real good guy, he says.

Here's a guy, I don't know, so-called best friend.

Laszlo lowers his voice but I can still hear him. He's too close to her. This is a guy that. Feed him breakfast. Pick him up, take him to work. Give him a job and uh, *float* him. And uh, my mom has his cheque, some deductions of course, he looks at it, something's wrong, he says.

The young woman asks Laszlo a question.

Yeah, my mom, she had it. And he stole! He stole from us! Laszlo cuts the air with a flat hand. I went by the next day. This is not the agreed. . . . What is this – this, this holding company? None of your business. Well, I said. I was ready to kill –

The dark-eyed woman breaks into his story.

Sorry, she says, I *really* have to run. Give me a call, she says. Gotta go!

Oh, he says. A-O-KAY! he says brightly. Laszlo tries to get funnier after the serious story. He needs a fast transition. He picks up her key ring, a tiny flashlight hooked on it, and he sings into the tiny flashlight as if it's a microphone: I DID IT MY WAY! he belts out.

My Funny Valentine, he croons softly, eyebrows up like Elvis Costello.

They both try to laugh but still she takes her keys back, plunging them deep within her Peruvian satchel.

The young woman leaves briskly, outside to oaks up like oars in a spooky sky, and Laszlo glances around, ill at ease now, alone, no longer singing. Now he has to adjust himself, recast the last moments, her exit. His status has changed here. He peers around at the subterranean concrete tomb as if for the first time, at the monotonous hockey draft unscrolling on the monster TV screen. It's a crap shoot. Some of us are wanted in the first or second round. Some players wait all day and no one calls. I'm not flying down east for nothing, for crocodile tears in the arena seats and maybe your parents phoning your hotel room, telling you there's next year, or you could play in Italy or Blackpool. Everyone will lie to you at some point. They decide they know best. Some are allowed dignity; others scramble. I will scramble if necessary. I'm not 6'5" but I'll run my cranium into the Zamboni if that's what they desire. They can croon my name, tap me on the shoulder, and I'll get it done. Only connect. Call my name. I'm shallow. I want to hear my muddled name run through a silver microphone, to shake hands with a million people I don't know.

Laszlo shows the red-haired bartender something from his wallet. A sunlit photo, waterfront property, a speedboat docked. The speedboat has a blue canopy and a blue racing stripe.

Looksee, he says. Is that a nice place or is that a nice place? Just up island. Hey, tell you what. You want to go there, let me know. I'm driving up there practically every week. All the goddamn time.

He carries a photo of property in his wallet. Now: would I be any different? I'd probably carry a photo too.

Laszlo scribbles a note left-handed, passes it over. The bartender does not read the note. I order a Greyhound, bite from the small onion I always carry in my coat. I'd like some chowder or chili, some good cornbread or sweet potato. Carbohydrate loading just in case I get picked.

Laszlo points with his sterling silver pen at the bartender's red hair.

You must be Irish, eh?

No, says the red-haired bartender, looking irritated.

Our place up island: we've got ten acres, two hundred grand. Bay goes in like this – we own from this peak to here. Goes back, big trees. Ten acres. Laszlo keeps smoking. He opens his wallet again. He likes to open his wallet. The ferry system, this is how. . . . The schedule. Thursday. No, hold that. Tuesday. Right. You know why Tuesday?

He lights another smoke. Dull Clapton plays: post-heroin Clapton, post-lobotomy Clapton. I'm truly sorry his little kid fell out of the high-rise but I don't like the tape. I like Art Bergman's new single: *create a monster, something something, we got a contract, contract, who's using who?* Art Bergman, crown prince of detox. The hockey draft is still on the screen. My draft. I'm so close to a contract, to treasure. Mr. Eric Clapton sells a billion boring records and no one wants me. The bartender doesn't ask why Tuesday.

On TV men in suits argue and wave clean hands en route to the silver microphone; they must speak their pick, announce who will skate, who will consider a million seven, who will buy a sleek growling speedboat. Something is wrong though; men in suits argue like they're chewing a mouthful of bees. They act as if they don't know their pick. I'm available! I shoot out mental telepathy messages from this edge of the country. Me! I have a head on my shoulders.

The erudite GM bends over; he seeks the ear of the frowning coach. The GM straightens, walks to talk with the worried head scout, then puts glasses on the end of his nose, peers over some papers. A weird delay of some kind, a plot complication at the meat market. Just past the media tables I can see the cackling old owner who was jailed for fraud and mob connections, for taking the Fifth, for taking the assets, for chortling. Well, no one figured he was a choirboy.

They'll take a d-man, says one customer.

No, they need a centre. Definitely a centre, says another.

The GM at the mike finally mouths the name of the anointed, the chosen. A goalie! Takes a goalie! They have goalies in the system. They have goalies coming out the yin yang. Trade bait, but who? Trade the young guy? The backup goalie? Trade the older goalie, the former cokehead?

They screwed up, someone in the bar says. They screwed up. He says this four times in a row.

They've been tricked. They traded up to get the franchise bruiser they wanted; they made a deal, and all parties agreed to square dance, to give and take. They agreed what bodies would be available when they got to the microphone but at the last second another team, a team without scruples, traded draft choices and future considerations, snatching the franchise bruiser out from under their red noses. Stole from them. Their *property*.

We've been snookered, states the GM, we've been submarined. The GM's Byzantine manoeuvres and agreements are useless. I traded up for nothing, he thinks, all that trouble for another goalie. The troubled scout tears the bruiser's name off their jersey, his sweater waiting at their table. How sure they were. They don't have my name on a jersey. They have different tables for each team, like it's the United Nations, like it's the fate of the free world. Then there are prickly-pear and sea lions, sooty terns and albatrosses and California sea lions dripping in the sun on the colour TV. Another highly illogical car commercial that seems to be selling something other than cars. What exactly is it they are hawking? Nature? Oceanfront? Does it work? Does it actually sell cars?

Insects crash at the screen, hearkening tragically into their multi-hued harbour. They want to eat the TV light, the only game in town. I keep studying the draft but Laszlo studies two women who seat themselves at the bar. The first woman keeps her sunglasses on. She is taller than me. I see her and think *stature, presence.* Her friend is shorter, with lighter hair and the small peaceful face of a follower.

The woman in the dark glasses inhales hugely, exhales: Well, we broke up. Went pretty well considering.

Woman #2: No sobbing?

Woman #1: A little. (She pauses.) Him. Not me.

Woman #2: Let's go prowling!

Woman #1: No thanks.

Woman #2: Oh yeah. You're in THAT phase. Wait two weeks and you'll be crawling the walls.

Woman #1: No. I don't think so.

I realize she has someone lusty waiting, someone already drafted, but she hasn't told her friend. She broke it off with one guy to move to another. She possesses a five-year plan. Woman #2 complains, My roommates are doing it all the time and I have to sit and listen. I mean I can't help but hear it. I can't afford my own place. And he has to end up with *her.* I had such a crush on him. It was supposed to be *me.* I had hopes. Now I'm going nuts. Why do I have such bad luck with guys I like?

They sip their drink specials.

Woman #1 says, This older guy took me to an Icelandic film festival. The movies were like, what the fuck!?

AHA! An older guy is chosen.

For me the charm of hockey was always its lack of charm. It wasn't hip. My agent says he'll call me back. He's busy with his "real" clients. I walk to the washroom and see a nickel gleaming at the bottom of the porcelain urinal. I do not pick it up. I look out at my nation. I have no nation. Okay – I have a wormwood nation.

Laszlo is talking to the two women: We'll take my Dad's speedboat across. If you don't have tackle we can get you some. Waterfront. On the water. Everyone said we paid too much. Local yokels laughing. Day later, $20,000 more. Who's laughing now? Very rare find. Very rare. Nice beach. Arbutus and oak. Beautiful property. We'll get some people. We'll go up there. Road trip! Road trip!

Well now, isn't waterfront always on the water? Woman #2 wonders.

What's the catch? I wonder. Why does Laszlo have to cajole people to go to this Shangri-La? Doesn't it come stocked with beautiful people? The way they stock a fish farm? A fat farm?

I realize Laszlo is talking to a different bartender. Bartender #2.

Bob Hope, Laszlo exclaims. Bob Hope's been there. We'd just fumigated so he wasn't too happy. Log cabin, some bugs. Ants, I guess. Cedar. Wouldn't think so. Puzzling. That loser shirt, Laszlo says, laughing at the bartender.

Hey sport. Hey pal. This is my brother's shirt. My brother who died in an accident. A *fatal* accident.

Oh. Sorry.

Laszlo lights another smoke, looks around. On TV a GM slides right by a team's table, a team he used to coach. He jumped ship. He doesn't look and they don't look at him. He found the loophole he needed to break his contract, to dance with another party, a party other than the one that "brung" him.

Bob Hope's a card. Bob Hope says, Any chance of anything here? Something other than pinochle and Ovaltine? Nyuck. Know what I mean? Country girls, nice country girls. He wanted some action. Horny old bugger. We caught a cod. Engine broke down, going slow, get a blueback, keeper, three-pounder, eat salmon that night. But I'd rather catch one big one. One big Chinook, a tyee, a king. Bob Hope bitching at me all day in that irritating voice. I'm looking for this ledge, I'm looking for this ledge with a depth finder. Jigged, buzz-bombed, mooched, nothing. Tried a new lure, a silver one I found in Dad's tacklebox.

(Now it's Bartender #3 half-listening, a guy in a muscle shirt. I think the bartenders must take shifts with Laszlo, then go hide back in the cooler.)

ZING! GOT IT! Laszlo mimics a fishing rod and a sudden strike on the line. ZING! He doesn't finish the fishing story. He smokes non-stop. I have another Greyhound. Maybe they don't draft players who punch their coaches. Maybe there's a secret agreement, rules they don't tell you about. I'm bitter (wormwood, wormwood). I'm starting to feel like saussurite, like schist, like stone.

A stoned voice bellows in the direction of the jukebox: PLAY SOMETHING . . . BY SOMEBODY . . . WHO KILLED THEMSELVES!

This desire to be fucked up, and think it something special, something to be attained. That's rich. Ask my friend Ryan if he's happy now.

All my friends are lawyers, Laszlo says. And the women are incredible! They work so hard they don't have time to meet anyone else. You want to meet great women, hang out with lawyers.

Yeah. Like I really want to hang out with lawyers, Bartender #3 growls.

On TV the GM in the suit is helping the young hockey player pull on his new team sweater. It's too intimate. There is some awkward tugging at clothes, then embarrassed smiles and camera flashes for the sports cards.

Who's this clown they pick? Who's this sack of hammers?
Some Swede faggot. A *foreigner*.
You on a team? Laszlo asks the muscled bartender.
Used to be. Same old used to be.
Now I recognize Bartender #3: a fantastically shifty forward
with Tri-Cities. He had moves like a humpback salmon, and
Pittsburgh was after him until he was submarined, blew out
both knees big time. Good old Tom what's-his-name. They said
he'd never walk again. Huge writhing scars each side of his
knees. Twins. A suicide pass. Skate into the middle and CRANG!
you flip over with a quicksilver crunching, then they carry you
off, a sudden screeching pauper. Wheelbarrows of cash will alter
anyone, but he's been changed by the cash he never got, by what
could have been that draft year. He could have been the one
under the blinding television lights, the one getting offered a
million seven. Instead. Well, instead he watches with me. Now
Tom what's-his-name is a major drunk with rehab muscles. I'm
not as shifty but at least my knees are okay. My knees are not too
shabby. I cast a shadow, I get my back up, show up for every
game. Buffalo could take me. The Jets. There's that windy corner. The Sharks. This sounds like *West Side Story*.

I'm going to drive up there to the property tomorrow. Come on
along. Pick up my cousin and bullshit. Deli grub, some
Heineken. Greenies. You like Heineken? No? The airport and
take the speedboat across.
Laszlo has told three different bartenders about the speedboat.
Laszlo asks, How does that bear joke go again? Let's see.
Bartender tells the bear he can't serve him because he's on drugs.
This part. I can never remember. Drugs. What drugs. You help
me, yeah. Oh, the *barbiturate*. The bar-bitch-you-ate! Ya ya. Ha
ha. That's a good one.
The two women do not share Laszlo's love of the bear joke.
We're lucky, you know, Laszlo says to the women, that place
up island. Played our cards right. Cheap locals can go jump in a
lake. If they knew anything they'd be somewhere else, right?
Road goes around pretty little bay. Speedboat. No waiting. Catch

a big one. No tackle we'll take care of you. Little general store not far. Good beef jerky. If we don't have it you don't need it. That's what they say on their sign. They don't have it you don't need it. That's their hick philosophy, their London School of Economics approach to local yokel marketing. Road goes around a nice little bay. See the smooth golden stones at the bottom. A beautiful place. We own it. It's ours.

Lizard King Jim Morrison says hello. Jim Morrison says he loves me. Morrison says he wants to know my name. The jukebox decides what to play. And the big screen shows the famous footage: Big surly Eric Lindros refuses the sweater. He stares off, dark mad eyes and curly hair. A thick neck, a bull. He'll never sign with this team. Maybe they called his name but that doesn't mean they own him, that doesn't mean he's their *property*. He refuses their blue uniform, their lovely stone city, their scheming owner. In this hexed process, this amateur hour crapshoot, here's what I wish to know, to *divine*: who has the real power and who is the victim? That's what I have to learn, even though I already know the truth.

Wait until Lindros is on the ice, the young man says to Bartender #4. He'll pay then. Someone'll stick him good. Get his bad knee.

I say nothing. He shouldn't talk like that. I've seen too many torn-up knees. Hurt!? Are you fucking kidding? Un-fucking-believable. Anterior cruciate; that's the worst. It digs into my stomach just thinking of ruined knees.

Just how many bartenders are back there? Do they have a bartender *pool*? There are more bartenders than customers.

Everyone thinks Lindros is a greedy arrogant asshole but meanwhile the team's owner is mulling over juicy offers of $75 million U.S. for the franchise. The Quebec owner will sell in the night; the owner will hustle the team out of Canada with a tearful press conference. The owner will cry all the way to the bank. Who's the greedy asshole then? What did our pal Peter Pocklington get for selling Gretzky to Los Angeles, for selling a person, a *human being*? $20 million? (For he is an honourable man.) And how much money does Peter the meatpacker owe the

Alberta government right now? He's in so deep they can't touch his house of cards, his dead pigs and stuffed sausages and offal, his slit-throat palace over the river valley. So the players are greedy? The players are arrogant? Give me a break. Get real.

No one gives me a break. No one gets real. Instead they draft a dead guy. In fact they draft Ryan, my friend from Salmon Arm. His last night on earth we were riding in what journalists would later refer to as the death car. I was passed out in the back seat. Ryan was in the passenger seat. Then I woke up in the ditch, in the rhubarb where the world was utterly different. Green water was pouring out of the upside-down radiator, burning me. The power pole was in three pieces, its line sparking. Ryan's head rolled across the gravel road, his brain still sending messages, questions, trying to find out what was wrong. I took off my wet shirt and hid my friend's head. I was afraid to pick it up so I just covered it with my shirt. What would you do? The car looked like modern sculpture, the driver still curled inside it like a foetus. Not a scratch on me, though my teeth were chattering and my hair was steaming. My friend's head: pebbles and dust stuck on it. And this brain of mine. Then some kind of gleaming milk truck came by and the driver said Jesus. And the big club must not know he's dead. If Ryan was alive he'd laugh. Here they are throwing away a pick on him before they'll draft me.

I have watched the drunken screen for hours, eating the past, wrapping my head in it and my eyes complain at the images, at the labour; my eyes are shifting right out of focus. Can't they make a big screen that doesn't kill you?

I am one of God's creatures but no one is taking me. Not the Lightning in Tampa, not the Panthers. Not the Jets. Not the San Jose Sharks. They're taking hundreds of snipers, killers, muckers, headcases, piranhas, pretenders. They call out polyglot Latvian names at the silver microphone. They don't care about my plus-minus, they don't care about my grade eight blues records or sensitive feelings or that I move like silt and stick like glue. What about the San Diego Gulls or Las Vegas and that Russian guy named Radek Bonk? This is a great name for a player. Bonk! Pass me the puck! Hit him, Bonk. Bonk him! Marty McSorley was going to sign with Las Vegas, play in the desert. I'd play in the desert. I can't go back to the fucking last-place Cougars. I know I'm *this* close to making it but the Cougars have dragged me down, they've buried me, made me invisible. In a seething minute you are made to pay for your geography, for being in the snake-bit boonies; the centre doesn't hold for *you*.

I'll have to try my luck as a free agent. Some good players aren't picked but they make it later as a walk-on. They force the issue, bull their way in the door. Courtnall, Joey Mullen, Dino Ciccarelli, Adam Oates, and that guy on the Habs. It happens. Brett Hull wasn't taken until the 117th pick, and Fleury was 166th his year. Nemchinov didn't go to New York until the 244th pick overall in 1990. Now he has a Stanley Cup ring. Every Cup team has its free agents, its "difficult" players. They made it, crawled out of the ooze. You hear their names: a mantra repeated. There's a free-agent camp somewhere in the States; the scouts look you over, look inside your head, see what you've got. Courtnall has it made in the shade now, big money, owns restaurants and a spiffy log cabin on a cliff over the crashing ocean. Douglas fir and ferns and fishing boats in the harbour where the whales come in to rub. A view. This is Geoff, not Russ. Russ was drafted first round and he married a movie starlet; Russ Courtnall has no idea what it's like to be invisible, to wait all day and be slowly made crazy, to want to punch out a guy named Laszlo. I'm so close, so close to treasure. Is it a litmus test, Russ? No. It's not a litmus test. Just look inside your rolling head, the head and source of all your son's distemper.

I wish the woman with dark eyes hadn't left. Why does one person seem different and necessary? I chose to interpret the angle of her neck, slurred messages the speed of blood inside her unknown neck and uncertain smile, her teeth and her lips with the darkest darkest lipstick. I watched the draft while I watched her eyes move, her brain shift into an uncertain smile, and I knew she was leaving just then to become a bus window or a blur in the rain in the raw city of colours, just as I knew I would not be drafted, as I knew they would take a dead man before they would take a player who clocked a coach.

On the Cougars Geoff punched anyone who touched his little brother Russ. I bet now both brothers bomb around in righteous speedboats, ocean their blue and white freeway while a pretty woman from Hollywood naps down in the V-berth. She is waiting for you and you are waiting for her. You are waiting to catch a big one. You stand wide-legged at the wheel and gaze at the sky over arbutus trees and your hair slides back in the salt breeze. You think your head is attached to your shoulders. Expensive sunglasses protect your eyes, zinc your fair skin, for you cast a shadow, you are the paragon of animals, you have connected the dots. Frantic lawyers and children clamour for your signature, your autograph; children and lawyers shout out your name in the sonic echoing arenas, in Inglewood, in Florida, in United Centre, in General Motors Place.

There is money moving out there, green as absinthe, green as antifreeze, and everyone has a chance at it. Take this from this, if this be otherwise.

That's the *system*. You think they are going to change it just for you?

ANNE SIMPSON

Dreaming Snow

I used to read books about polar exploration. Sometimes I doodled in the margins of Fridtjof Nansen's Arctic journal, thinking of the three-masted boat keeled over slightly to starboard, fixed fast in the ice, yet moving imperceptibly with it, as it drifted from Siberia towards Greenland over the frozen polar sea, and of the men inside it, sitting in the warm, brightly lit saloon, playing backgammon, perhaps, or chess. After a while, I knew passages by heart and sometimes changed the words, rewriting it in a notebook which was a compendium of dreams, bits of fact, and odd visions. I saw it in my own way, entire in its strangeness, complete, a tale of dreaming words.

A door banged wildly against the side of the house. Aunt Maura never thought to fasten the screen door when she came in.

I would have had doubts starting off on a voyage like that, standing at the rail, watching the land recede into mist, in all its spectrum of colours, transparent mauves and blues, soft gauzy greys, moisture that lighted out of the air, stinging the skin briefly.

July 24, 1893 – The Fram glides away from the press of people on the quay, little dabs of colour jostling together before they darken and diminish. A young woman appears in a rowboat holding a parasol, waving an embroidered handkerchief as she is obscured by mist, and for a moment only the handkerchief is visible before it, too, vanishes. On the starboard side there is a red dory, containing a golden retriever, a boy, and an old man in a makeshift wheelchair strapped to the thwarts. The old man holds up an oar and shouts something we can't make out; he disappears as swiftly as the young woman. In another boat a man in a stiff white collar stands, cheering for Nansen: "It is a great day for Norway, surely a great day. Gå fram." We float on, hovering, through silvery veils, as if there is nothing but air under us, hearing far off the staccato of the gun salute from Christiana; simultaneously, near our bows, two boats collide. A skiff overturns and two young men have to be rescued. Garbled, excited voices rise on all sides, and then fade away. We veer to the lee to avoid a startled fisherman rearing up like a walrus from the half-deck of his boat, and slip into an unearthly silence, into a vague grey in which there is no horizon, only the breakwater as a marker, which we steam past. There are tears in Fridtjof's eyes as he turns to me: "So Hjalmar; we begin." It seems to me that the mist hangs with a clinging moistness, heavy as drapes.

Aunt Maura came in to ask how I was, poor thing, such a time of it I'd had, and how was the baby today. Then she took Samuel out of his bassinette, in which he was making contented mewing sounds, and cuddled him close, with the practised hands of one who knew how to hold an infant. I wanted to hold him – I loved the touch of his warm skin, fragrant with a milky smell – but Aunt Maura told me to sleep while she fed him and put him down properly, in his own Mister Master Samuel crib, in his own wee small room. I lay back, exhausted. When Gareth came home later I could hear them talking quietly in the kitchen. Aunt Maura's sentences rose at the end, and he responded with a longer reply, which wound in and out. They were talking about me.

Gareth brought me tea and for some reason the sight of his warm face – his hair tousled because he had yanked a sweater off – brought tears to my eyes. He was interrupted by the sound of Samuel crying and went to get him, putting him down on the bed close to me. He tickled the tiny feet. Then he took my hand

and put it on Samuel's velvety head; my fingers splayed out as if in blessing.

July 28, 1893 – Within a day or so we will sight Novaya Zemlya. They will sight it first, because I am feeding the boiler's golden tiger flames. I shovel the coal until the fire blossoms up in a jungle of white-gold, orange, blue. I recall each word Fridtjof says to me, his jokes, his remarks; I laugh when he tells me that I have the eyes of a sad English sheepdog, when he calls me his good lieutenant, Hjalmar, and thumps me on the back. I watch him instructing Pettersen about cleaning the engine cylinders, marvelling at his ease. Then he climbs the ladder to the saloon, humming as he goes. He doesn't realize his stoker is a woman who is restless, ghostly, thinking of Fridtjof's hands on her skin, on her throat, along the length of her legs. I am a fire, flickering.

In the night, I turned my head to look at Gareth, lying on his side of the bed, with an arm over his face. When we made love we used to rock back and forth vigorously, holding each other. Everywhere I touched him it seemed that my fingers were made of light, leaving bright signatures on his skin. But now, lying on the white sheet, my arms loosely over my head, I could have been lying on a drift of snow.

I woke to the sound of crying.

July 29, 1893 – Late in the evenings Fridtjof sits alone in his cabin, where he has pinned up delicate pencil drawings of his wife and smooth-faced child, which he has sketched himself. He writes; yearning for Eva, always Eva. Then he scribbles over what he has written – I know what he has written – about her white arms, her shining hair, the movements of her hands, her quick fingers, when she is kneading bread.

Gareth took Samuel gently from me and warmed a bottle for him in the kitchen.

I lay awake, afraid to sleep again. I thought of a green country, knit with lanes and hedges, with dusky plums clinging to branches, windfall apples in the ditches. I remembered toiling uphill on a bicycle. It was early September, the sky a mild, changeable blue, and I was on my way to Wales. By the time I arrived in Llangollen, everything was steeped in honey-coloured light. I was tired and didn't want to talk to anyone in the youth hostel, not the German teenagers, not the man reading in a soft, frayed armchair, feet propped on a stool, eating a mashed banana in a chipped bowl. In his canvas knapsack was a wooden recorder. I thought he was a native Welshman. His hair was a kind of red-gold colour like a Pre-Raphaelite hero or an Irish setter, and I had a peculiar desire to walk over and touch it. I sat watching him, eating my sandwich and soup, curious to know what he was reading. He continued to read, occasionally clinking the spoon against the bowl, and didn't look up.

When he hiked up a footpath through the hills the next morning, I followed, finally catching up with him. He told me his name, shyly, slowly – "Gaar-reth" – and said he was from North Carolina, from a little place called Pye's River. He held his hand out stiffly. As he spoke I realized I wanted to lie down on the ground with him and make love. He was thinking the same thing. I felt it in my fingertips, which I hid in my pockets.

July 30, 1893 – We are waiting to reach the Yugor Strait; all of us tense because we have encountered ice where we didn't expect it. And there is a thick fog, so thick that it is hard to distinguish one man from another. We try to move through the ice when the fog lifts: Sverdrup spins the wheel hard starboard, then hard to port, then back again, anxious about handling the boat in the ice, until the bow runs up on it and bursts it underneath. The noise is deafening. "She's a real ice-boat," laughs Sverdrup, "rolling over it like a ball on a platter." After a day of this we are out of the ice; the fog lifts and the evening is clear. In the small hours of night, I climb the rigging and stand in the crow's nest, a hundred feet or more above the water. I am loose and free up here, suspended. There is a curl of moon, a thin peeling of light. But my hands are trembling. Last night, when I tried to talk to Fridtjof in the chart room, he turned away to check whether there was moisture in the theodolite.

*Below the crow's nest, far below, the water flickers, beckons. . . .
When we reach Khabarova, which is flat and grey, I am terribly
unhappy. There is nothing in this landscape.*

Samuel was sleeping when Gareth left in the morning. I picked
up my notebook, but there was nothing to write. I looked out the
window. There was still snow, which, in late April, lay in dirty
patches by the shed. The garden was mottled and brown, full of
the bent stalks of dead plants. Beyond the shed, the ice had disappeared from the bay, which made the steel-blue water even
more forbidding. The spruce trees lifted and sagged in the wind.

When I looked down, there were triangles and loops drawn
around the name "Fridtjof Nansen" on the page. I saw him
clearly all of a sudden: a brown woollen hat low over his eyebrows, with reddish-brown hair curling out from behind his
ears, a plaid scarf, and a faint scent on his skin that might have
been buttered toast. After a moment or two, I lay down and
pulled the covers up, wishing I were small again, like Samuel.

I grew up in Glace Bay, youngest in a family of eight. My mother
was Portuguese and she loved singing as much as cooking, so
that whatever she cooked was full of love and devotion, full of
her vibrant, floating voice. My father had once wanted to be a
priest, before he settled into his life's work of selling snow-
mobiles. He worried about me: when I fell out of the oak tree, he
ran to where I lay sprawled on the grass, asking, in a confused,
strangled voice, whether anything was broken, putting his ear to
my heart, without thinking to check my bones.

My brother Samuel took care of us all when we were children, straightening my hair ribbons in church, blacking Derek's
shoes for school, helping with the store accounts on Sunday
evening. My father relied on him, my mother tousled his hair
even when he was seventeen and going out with girls, and I
adored him. He and I were full of the same wildness, though in
my case it had been tamped down. He was the one who found me
when I took John Whybrow's rowboat and tried to row it to
China, before I got stuck in the weeds by Mr. Burleigh's dock. He

walked me home after that, never saying a word about it being a silly thing to do, only that I had been heading in the wrong direction for China.

Samuel was going to marry Christa MacChesney when he turned twenty-one. He knew this, Christa knew this, and I knew this, because I heard them talking about it on the front porch. I disliked Christa. I didn't like the way she looked at him. But that was before she met James Irving Morey and got all mooney-eyed over him, so that I wanted to pull her hair out, strand by strand. But Samuel would sit for hours without doing anything and then get up and go hunting in his old red half-ton truck. He drove clear across the Trail to Cheticamp one day and didn't come back until evening.

October 9, 1893 – We are on the ice floe now, encased in ice, throttled by it . . . it glistens all around, stretching for miles in pure, excruciating whiteness, painful to look at, unless the eye falls on the shadows, which are mauve and blue. We drift through white space.

A deafening noise begins, and the whole boat shakes, lifted up with the pressure, high up. The noise subsides. And then it begins again, with a cracking, a moaning, which gradually increases . . . for a while it is a high plaintive sound, then low grumbling, as it steadily becomes louder: an organ played by a madman. It stops abruptly. There is an eerie sound, a long drawn-out note of pure pain; the cry of a woman.

It is quiet until the dogs begin howling; they are frightened, turning around and snapping at the air.

On Samuel's nineteenth birthday my mother made apple-blueberry pancakes and sausages, as a special treat. The warm, sweetish smell of pancake batter wafted from the griddle, mingled with the strong, slightly bitter smell of coffee. My sister Kathryn was playing a Strauss waltz on the piano in the sitting room. Samuel and my mother began to waltz around the table until my father switched on the radio and Kathryn immediately stopped playing. Through the scratchy static we heard that Yvan Cournoyer had scored a crucial goal for the Habs in the third period. My mother and Samuel stopped, her arm in a flamboyant gesture above her head. They stayed there for a moment or two: rigid and perfect. I flipped the pancakes, watching them. Then my mother began to laugh. Theresa Anne knocked her dish from her high chair to the floor and started howling.

October 11, 1893 – It is Pettersen's birthday and we are all celebrating. Bentzen plays "Napoleon's March Across the Alps" on the accordion and Juell begins to clump around the saloon in his clogs, doing a jig. He invites Fridtjof to join him and they stamp around the floor like boys until Juell falls at the galley door. They don't pay any attention to the cracking of the ice, when the pressure builds again, but I leave them to go back up to the deck. I can see with clarity because of the moonlight; each time the ice rumbles it seems that it will split the boat apart. On the port side, the ice rises in a ridge and then there is an explosion as it breaks apart. Fridtjof has come on deck during this spectacle and stands beside me on the foredeck, looking out. He smokes a pipe and I shape words of love in my mind; they are the sounds of the ice breaking and knifing into pieces.

The winter Samuel turned nineteen was unusually cold. One day in February it was so bitter that when I went out to feed the chickens, I got frostbite on the tips of my fingers where there were holes in my mittens. The snow squeaked underfoot and my eyelashes stuck together. Samuel didn't come back for supper and I was still awake waiting for him at midnight. I went out to the sitting room, where my father was staring out a dark window and my mother sat with her crocheting on her knees. In the morning, Samuel still hadn't come home. That evening the priest from Our Lady of the Sea came by the house. The mountie at Cheticamp had telephoned him: they had found my brother. My mother began to rock back and forth as he told my parents, in that slow, kindly voice of his, that my brother was being sent to St. Martha's Hospital, and that he might not make it through the night. Father Anthony refrained from saying that

they used a screwdriver to pry open the frozen door on the
driver's side of the truck, parked at the look-out on French
Mountain, and that there was a half-empty bottle of Captain
Morgan between my brother's legs, which spilled as they moved
him, so that the smell of it must have been rich, and rank, as
skunk.

He made it through the night. That night, and all the days and
nights that followed, my mother stayed with him, saying her
rosary over and over. The decision was made to amputate his left
hand, which my parents did not resist; later, both feet and the
other hand were amputated. A few weeks later he died.

*January 3, 1894 – It is pitch dark when there is no moon – there
is only the faintest glow of hidden sunlight for a brief time each
day. I am walking with Fridtjof on the floe, pausing occasionally as he checks the sounding equipment. Above us the northern lights are waving, folded bands of silver, changing to yellow,
then green, then red. Fridtjof stands quite still looking up, but
the colour diminishes. Then to the south it begins again with a
few streamers of faint violet; these begin to waver across the sky
in a series of soft pleats. There are hues of rose and pale yellow,
rippling like silk in the darkness.*

*It is a dream about my life, other lives, all those who had
lived before me, stretched out like a band of colours. I see my
own life like a shimmering, changing thread, but it is mixed in
with all the others.*

"How would you describe it, Hjalmar?" Fridtjof asks me.

Gareth and I lived in an old house with a faulty woodstove at
Maiden Cove. The first Christmas he ordered an electric stove
out of the Sears catalogue so I could bake things to sell. When I
baked, I devoted myself utterly to the process, kneading bread
the way some people make love: strong, firm movements of my
hands, not too hard, but just enough. The cakes were invariably
light as air, and they tasted delicious, but always faintly pungent
and spicy; a taste people couldn't quite describe, even though
they tried. That was the way it should be, to keep people guess-
ing, my mother had taught me.

After a year and a half of saving my baking money in large pickle bottles in the pantry, I went to an auction at St. Jerome's Bay and bought a washer, a television, a crib, and a rocker. My belly was full and round by then. I marvelled at the way the skin stretched drum-tight over the baby's head. The sun slanted through the window in early April, pouring over the cat's back as it lay in the rocker, filling the petals of the rosy cyclamen on the window sill so that it glowed. I stood by the sink in the window's warmth: I was ready, the child was ready. A few days later, I woke with pains in my back. I didn't wake Gareth. I got up and began ironing shirts, a red pleated skirt, a frilly nightgown. The pain seemed to come and go without any particular pattern. I watched a young man waver on the screen as he talked about a low pressure system, and when he pointed to a red and orange circle that was covering part of New Brunswick, I cried out.

The labour lasted through one full day and another night. The baby was born early in the morning of the second day: small, bloody, and floured with something whitish, which made him ugly. But I thought he was radiant, beautiful. The nurses cleaned him, wrapping him in striped flannel, so that he resembled a small loaf of freshly baked bread. I held out my arms as Gareth handed me our son, Samuel.

February 11, 1894 – "I write about these lights often," says Fridtjof, looking up, "but I can never capture it." He pauses for a moment, still craning his neck to look at the lights. Then he flashes a smile and I am surprised by the white of his teeth. "These are words," he says, gesturing, "written about love – all over the sky. But there is some sadness in it."

Giving birth seemed a strange thing, as though I had gone underwater, drowned, and come up to the surface. Finally, I lapsed into sleep again, dreaming that someone was touching my face. I kept my eyes closed as the fingers travelled, slowly, over my face, as if to identify features of geography. I waited until the ghost hands stopped moving. I was afraid of this dream, afraid to look into a face which I knew was tender, with the fineness of a girl's features. The eyebrows were lightly drawn, the nose narrow, and the eyes dark blue. My brother's face. The hands stopped moving, as though something had happened, as if they had been arrested by some discovery.

I woke with deep, fierce pains in my body.

June 30, 1894 – Fridtjof is making plans to leave the Fram some-time in the early spring of next year. I believe that he will take only one companion with him. It is sure to be Scott-Hansen. I have seen them talking together for hours as they fish for algae in the small pools by the Fram.

It has become much too bright; the summer light exhausts me.

For a week after I haemorrhaged, the nurses gave me pills in lit-tle plastic cups and I took them meekly, tiny capsules filled with something sour, metallic, to be swallowed with a glass of water. When the obstetrician came, she spoke mostly to Gareth and once in a while she would swing her head around to me. I was indifferent to her. It seemed as if I had been travelling for miles. Lifting my hand was a time-consuming task, as was turn-ing my head to look out the window. Gareth got up to leave, kiss-ing me on the forehead. I closed my eyes. Nothing bothered me. There was only the extraordinary weight of the darkness, heavy and deep as earth.

When I woke in the night, I imagined my mother sitting in the chair by the window, hunched over her rosary. I heard the papery sound of her whispers. I heard every prayer, over and over.

October 10, 1894 – Today is Fridtjof's birthday: he is thirty-three. We put a banner on his cabin door with the words, "Til lykke med dagen." In the morning several of us go skiing but it is colder than it has been in a long time, about –31 degrees Celsius. After dinner Blessing pulls out a bottle of Lysholmer liqueur, and from his pockets he takes measuring glasses, med-icine glasses, test glasses, giving each of us a dram or two.

Afterwards, I walk back and forth on the deck, watching for the polar bear that has been lurking about for the past few nights. Yesterday Fridtjof asked me to go with him when he strikes out for the North Pole. He asked me to think about it carefully because I would be risking my life. I swing my arms in circles to keep warm, thinking about whether I am afraid of dying.

After two weeks Gareth took me home. He put me on the burgundy sofa with a quilt over my knees and the cat on my lap, offering me steaming mugs of homemade soup. And he bathed Samuel in the kitchen sink as I watched, marvelling. But most of the time I slept in bed, deadened and empty. When Gareth went back to work, Aunt Maura appeared. She gave me oatmeal biscuits and tea, tucking in my blankets, telling me that Samuel was all curled up, sweet Sammums, and far away in dreamland.

When she left, I walked to the kitchen, shuffling like an old woman, and looked out the window at the sheets on the clothesline. The wind whipped the first sheet, so that it wound, tortured, around the line. One edge flipped in the wind. Samuel whimpered and I waited for a moment, listening. It was silent, except for the wind. After I'd made some tea and looked out the window again, all the sheets were tangled the same way over the line. I could see the cat playing with a field mouse which was not quite dead.

I put on my rubber boots and a coat over my nightgown, and went outside. I stood for a long time wondering what to do. Then I saw the sheets and remembered. It took quite a while to walk towards the clothesline, but then I wasn't sure if I could manage to get up on the sawhorse to free the sheets. When I tried, the pain was intense. I stood up on the sawhorse and released the first sheet. Then I got down, stepping back from it as it snapped in the wind. It flew up wildly, and as it did I could see an entire Arctic landscape spread out in front of me, silvery-white, shimmering. Then the sheet flapped down, obscuring it. I lifted a corner, expectantly, but everything was the same as it had always been. The path snaked down to the beach, the sea lay dark and calm.

I freed each sheet in turn, moving the sawhorse and climbing up on it each time, trembling with the effort. When I went back to the house, I saw that the cat had left part of the field mouse's body on the step at the back door.

March 14, 1895 – I take one last look at the Fram, which looks peculiar from this distance, slightly tilted. Its silhouette is so familiar to me: the strangely rounded hull, the three masts, the webs of rigging.

After we have travelled for about three hours, those who are staying with the Fram – Pettersen, Sverdrup, Scott-Hansen, and the others – shake hands with us. We say good-bye abruptly. There are tears in Pettersen's eyes and I feel empty when they turn away, awkwardly, on their skis. When they have gone a short distance, they wave and so do we, forcing ourselves to turn in the other direction.

Soon there is no thought of anything except keeping the dogs in line so that they don't tangle the traces. It is difficult to ski while managing the dogs and the sled at the same time. The wind is bitter, driving right into our faces, which makes it hard to breathe. I drive the sled behind Fridtjof, following blindly. We plunge into white nothingness.

I was having trouble measuring distances. In the night I bumped into the bookcase on the way to the bathroom and hit my shoulder, bruising it badly. I sat down in the hallway, still holding my shoulder, wondering at the pain. Nothing could be seen for miles, except a ridge of broken ice to the south. Then Gareth appeared. He didn't seem to be bothered by the cold. I was struck by the way he walked nonchalantly over the ice in his bare feet. I put my hands out to him and he helped me up. Then he carried me back to the bedroom. With the moonlight in stripes over his head, he was Fridtjof, and then, when he moved back into the shadow, he was Gareth again.

March 24, 1895 – It is storming and the wind is whipping in freezing blasts. It has become impossible to go on in the face of it. We tried setting up the tent but it blew down and Fridtjof only just managed to catch it before it blew away. We sit close to one another, as the dogs do, huddling for warmth. After an hour or so, the wind subsides, and we are able to put up the tent. But it is still bitterly cold. I start the stove and we heat a little broth and eat some chocolate but then we are both over-whelmed by the need to sleep. Fridtjof's eyes are closing, even as he bites into the chocolate. We sleep from six in the evening until nine o'clock the next day.

We exist for nothing else except making our way forward, always forward. Up and over one high ice ridge and then down, and after each ridge the dogs have to be sorted out. We have to take off our gloves to untangle the lines. All my energy is spent climbing and descending the ice ridges, trying not to break the sled or my skis.

April 5th – The ice conditions are making our journey extremely difficult. Already the first week of April has nearly passed. We are working our way further to the west, hoping that the hellish ice ridges will disappear, but the ice becomes more broken as we go, as if some giant had crumpled it in his fist. I long to lie down and sleep. This journey is almost more than I can bear.

We will not be able to go forward much further. The ice continues to get worse.

April 7th – 86 degrees, 14 minutes N. Fridtjof has decided that it is impossible to continue towards the Pole. We are turning back.

On top of the last ridge I see a rocking chair and a crib. The chair rocks slightly. We descend the broken ice, going south-west. I look back, but there is only a pressure ridge of ice.

April 29th – We have to kill another dog. Bruin is so weak that he can't even hobble. It is not easy to kill these beautiful ani-mals quickly, but we have to. The knife is no longer sharp, but I have learned precisely where to thrust it.

May 10th – We must kill the last dog today.

May 26th – Perhaps one day we will reach Spitzbergen. I hope I will not die here, with nothing around me. There is, I know, a reason why I must return, but I have forgotten what it is. My mind is playing tricks. I imagine that I am walking naked across the ice, that the cold does not affect me. I walk towards Fridtjof and he is also naked. He is not surprised by my body, which is shaped and curved like a woman's body. We lie together, side by side on the ice, without touching. He turns his head and I see Gareth's face.

We make love on the ice, which is surprisingly soft and warm underneath us. My fingers, as they touch his body, flicker with little flames.

May 30th – We should have reached Spitzbergen by now, unless we are further to the east than Fridtjof imagined. But we have sighted eider duck far off in the sky, so there must be land, though it evades us. Fridtjof is going off to the west to see if he can locate it. But I am suffering from the onset of snow blindness. I will stay here and sleep.

I wake to the sound of a Strauss waltz and when I unfasten the tent flaps, I see a girl – with braids like my sister's – sitting at a piano. My father is sitting on the burgundy sofa, turning the knobs of the radio on the walnut table beside him. Further away, where the ice is flat, my brother Samuel is dancing with my mother. She is wearing her long blue bathrobe which swirls around her like a ball gown. Her dark hair falls out of its bun and down to her waist, swinging as she dances. Both of them are laughing.

I hear something behind me and turn, thinking of bears, but it is a golden plover, beating its wings overhead.

June 5th – In the vague distance, in a haze of white, I think I can see Fridtjof returning, a dark figure making a wide detour around a pool of water. I ski towards him slowly, like someone in a trance. Perhaps he has found land.

I reach the last hummock of ice, unfasten my skis with difficulty and climb up, losing my balance now and then because of the mist over my eyes. When I haul myself to the top of the ridge, no one is there.

June 9th – I have spent two days looking for Fridtjof, to no avail. He must be dead. For some reason I feel no sadness.

June 14th – It is almost warm in the middle of the day and the ice is frequently a soft mush, making it difficult to ski. The dark shape on the horizon has become a solid mass. It is land – probably Franz Joseph Land – but it will still take time to get to it. It may not be land; I may be dreaming it.

June 19th – I have reached land. I leave the sled and skis behind, taking only what I need as I walk towards the southeast. It must be night, even though the sun is just going down. There is still a great deal of light so I keep walking, scraping my hands as I clamber over ice and rocks. The horizon is crimson for a while, until it softens to beaten gold. Some ivory gulls wheel above me.

There is much less ice the further I walk in this direction. I see stones on the beach, each one distinct. There are many birds overhead: some gulls, an eagle. The wind is from the south. It is strangely familiar.

June 22nd – In the distance, I see a small shed near the edge of the cliff. As I get closer, I see an old farmhouse. But I am dreaming the path winding up to it. I am dreaming the clothesline, the sheets snapping in the wind. Flowers curl out of the earth in brilliant colours.

I wait for it to disappear.

But it is still there. I see a woman working in the garden. Her dark hair is coiled up out of her eyes. She sits back on her heels for a moment and picks up a rattle for the baby lying on a plaid blanket. Her gaze is alert and calm.

As I move towards her I become lighter, so that I am nothing more than a breath of wind she feels for a moment, as it lifts her hair.

About the Authors

Brian Bartlett has published several collections of poetry, including *Granite Erratics* (Ekstasis, 1997) and *Underwater Carpentry* (Goose Lane, 1993). He is a two-time winner of the *Malahat Review* Long Poem Prize, most recently in 1997. Besides currently working on a novel and new poems, he has also embarked upon a book of essays, journals, and other prose pieces, *Living with Poetry*; parts of it have appeared in *The Antigonish Review*, *Books in Canada*, *Canadian Literature*, *The Fiddlehead*, and *Studies in Canadian Literature*. Bartlett teaches creative writing and literature at Saint Mary's University in Halifax.

Dennis Bock's first collection, *Olympia*, will be published by Doubleday Canada in the spring of 1998. He is currently working on a novel, *The Reading Boy*, which will be published by Bloomsbury in the U.K. He lives in Toronto, where he is co-fiction editor of *B&A new fiction*. The story included here will appear in Oberon's *Coming Attractions 1997*.

Gabriella Goliger lives in Ottawa. She is winner of the 1993 *Prism international* fiction award. Her story "Song of Ascent" appeared in the 1995 *Journey Prize Anthology* and was short-listed for the prize. She is currently working on a collection of stories that draws on her German-Jewish heritage.

Terry Griggs was born in Little Current, Manitoulin Island, and has recently returned there after living in London, Ontario, for several years. She has published a collection of short stories, *Quickening*, which was nominated for a Governor General's Award, and a novel, *The Lusty Man*. She is presently working on another novel, entitled *The Iconclast's Journal*, as well as a novel for children.

Kristen den Hartog was born in Deep River, Ontario, and now lives in Toronto. Her work has appeared in several literary magazines, including *Event, Other Voices, B&A new fiction*, and *The Antigonish Review*. Most recently, *Prairie Fire* published her story "Star," a sister story to "Wave." She is currently at work on *Flutterby*, a novel that stems from both these stories.

Mark Anthony Jarman was born in Edmonton, is a graduate of the Iowa Writers' Workshop, and now teaches English at the University of Victoria. He has published recently in *Hawaii Review, Passages North, McGill Street, Grain, Prism, Event, B&A, sub-TERRAIN, Rio Grande Review, Zygote, Queen's Quarterly*, and *Quarry*. A story, "California Cancer Journeys," will be included in 97: *Best Canadian Stories* (Oberon) and "Righteous Speedboat" will be published in *Our Game*, a hockey fiction anthology (Polestar). "Righteous Speedboat" will also appear in his new collection of stories in spring 1998. His first novel, *Salvage King Ya!*, was published by Anvil Press in 1997.

Judith Kalman's personal essay "Flight" won a Tilden Canadian Literary Award in 1995, as well as the National Magazine Award in personal journalism and the National Magazine Awards President's Medal in the same year. She has published stories in *Grain, Prairie Fire, Windsor Review, Queen's Quarterly*, and *Descant*, among other journals. "Not for Me a Crown of Thorns" will also appear in her book *The County of Birches*, a collection of linked short stories to be published by Douglas & McIntyre in the spring of 1998. She lives with her husband and two sons in Toronto.

Andrew Mullins is a Montreal writer. "The World of Science" is the first publication he will admit to. He is currently working on a collection of stories.

Sasenarine Persaud is the author of two novels, *The Ghost of Bellow's Man* (1992) and *Dear Death* (1989), three books of poetry, including *A Surf of Sparrows' Songs* (TSAR, 1996), and several essays, most recently, "Khevat: Waiting on Yogic

Realism," on yogic realism, a school he is pioneering. He won the K.M. Hunter Foundation's Emerging Artist Award (1996) for his story collection in manuscript form, *Canada Geese and Apple Chatney*. His work has appeared in journals and anthologies in Canada, England, the Middle East, the United States, and the West Indies. He is presently revising his latest book, *The Hungry Sailor*.

Anne Simpson lives with her family in Antigonish, Nova Scotia, where she paints and writes. She also teaches writing at the Learning Centre at St. Francis Xavier University. Her work has been published in *The Fiddlehead*, *Quarry*, *The Malahat Review*, and *Prism international*, among other journals. She has just finished writing a first novel, *Canterbury Beach*.

Sarah Withrow's short fiction has appeared in *The Fiddlehead* and will soon appear in *Descant*. She has just completed a novel for young adults, *Bat Summer* (in search of a publisher). She writes – for love and money – in Ottawa.

Terence Young is co-editor of *The Claremont Review*, a literary magazine for emerging writers aged thirteen to nineteen. He won *This Magazine*'s Great Canadian Literary Hunt in 1996 and was short-listed in the recent Writers' Union of Canada short-fiction contest for his story "Rhymes with Useless." His first collection of poetry, *Letters to an Absent Wife*, is forthcoming from Véhicule Press.

About the Contributing Journals

Border Crossings is a quarterly interdisciplinary magazine of the arts published in Winnipeg. A local, international magazine, *Border Crossings* covers all of the fine arts, including architecture, dance, photography, painting, film, theatre, poetry, and fiction. In its fifteen years of publication, *Border Crossings* has received more than eighty-eight nominations for National and Western Magazine awards and has been awarded twenty-nine medals. Described by *Globe and Mail* writer Robert Everett Green as "Canada's only magazine devoted to the next great thing in all the arts," *Border Crossings* brings the best art writing, the liveliest interviews, and the most thorough discussion of contemporary art and culture. Submissions: 500–70 Arthur Street, Winnipeg, Manitoba, R3B 1G7.

Descant is a quarterly literary magazine which publishes poetry, prose, fiction, interviews, travel pieces, letters, photographs, engravings, art, and literary criticism. Editor: Karen Mulhallen. Managing Editor: Mary Myers. Submissions and correspondence: P.O. Box 314, Station P, Toronto, Ontario, M5S 2S8.

The Fiddlehead, Canada's longest-living literary, appears quarterly and publishes both new and old writers, looking always for vitality, freshness, and surprise. Subscribers live in all parts of the globe, contributors mainly (though not exclusively) in Canada. We publish unsolicited poetry and short stories, but solicit book reviews. Editor: Bill Gaston. Submissions and subscription correspondence: Campus House, University of New Brunswick, P.O. Box 4400, Fredericton, N.B., E3B 5A3.

Grain "Food For Your Brain" magazine provides readers with fine, fresh writing by new and established writers of poetry and prose, four times a year. Published by the Saskatchewan Writers Guild, *Grain* has earned national and international recognition for its distinctive literary content. Editor: J. Jill Robinson. Prose Editor: Connie Gault. Poetry Editor: Tim Lilburn. Submissions and correspondence: Box 1154, Regina, Saskatchewan, S4P 3B4. E-mail: grain.mag@sasknet.sk.ca Web site: http://www.sasknet.com/corporate/skwriter

Matrix is a literary/cultural magazine rooted in Quebec but open to writers from across Canada, the United States, and abroad. Seeks out the best contemporary fiction, non-fiction, articles, and artwork. Described by Bill Katz, in *Library Journal*, as "a northern combination of *The New Yorker* and *Atlantic Monthly*." Publishes original prose and poetry by new and established writers. Length 1,500 to 5,000 words. Articles/fiction receive $100 to $200; poetry $15 to $100. Pays on publication. Guidelines available. Submissions and correspondence: 1400 de Maisonneuve W., Suite 514-8, Montreal, Que., H3G 1M8.

The New Quarterly publishes a lively and eclectic mix of fiction and poetry plus views from the inside of the writer's craft. A recent winner of both gold and silver medals for fiction at the National Magazine Awards and earlier of a silver medal for poetry, *The New Quarterly* shows off the work of new writers alongside that of veterans. Recent features include John Metcalf and the editor/writer relationship, Robyn Sarah on journal keeping, Diana Brebner's ideas on order and poetry, Steven Heighton on writing as a vocation in a virtual world, Katherine Govier on her life as a writer-in-residence, and James Gordon on singing those hometown blues. Good talk, a good read, and all at a good price! Submissions and correspondence: ELPP, PAS 2082, University of Waterloo, Waterloo, Ontario, N2L 3G1.

Other Voices is an Edmonton-based literary magazine which publishes two issues a year. It considers high-quality work from any perspective, from both new and established writers, particularly women. Its editors are interested primarily in fiction and non-fiction prose and poetry, but also welcome reviews and artwork. Submissions and correspondence: P.O. Box 52059, 8210–109 Street, Edmonton, Alberta, T6G 2T5.

Parchment welcomes unsolicited poetry and short fiction by Canadian writers on Jewish themes. Only items submitted in duplicate with sufficient postage on a return envelope will be considered. Subscription rates are $12 for one year and $20 for two years. Submissions and subscription requests: Parchment, Centre for Jewish Studies, Vanier 260, York University, 4700 Keele Street, North York, Ontario, M3J 1P3.

Pottersfield Portfolio is an independent tri-annual journal publishing fiction, poetry, essays, and book reviews. Founded in 1979, it accepts submissions from any geographical region and has published the work of Governor General's Award-winners along with writers publishing for the first time. The type of work published in *Pottersfield Portfolio* ranges across a broad spectrum from the traditional to the unusual and innovative. Editor: Ian Colford; Fiction Editor: Karen Smythe. Submissions and correspondence: P.O. Box 27094, Halifax, N. S., B3H 4M8. E-mail (for queries only): saundc@auracom.com Web site: http://www.auracom.com/~saundc/potters.html

Prism international has published, for more than thirty years, work by writers both new and established, Canadian and international. Edited by graduate students of creative writing at the University of British Columbia, *Prism* looks for innovative fiction, poetry, drama, as well as creative non-fiction, in English or English translation. The 1997-98 editorial board will consist of Sara O'Leary as Editor; Sioux Browning and Melanie Little as Co-editors; and Shannon McFerran as Executive Editor. *Prism* also holds an annual fiction contest. Request guidelines or send submissions to: The Editors, *Prism international*, Department of Creative Writing, BUCH E462–1866 Main Mall, University of British Columbia, Vancouver, B.C., V6T 1Z1. E-mail: prism@unixg.ubc.ca Web site: http://www.arts.ubc.ca/crwr/prism/prism.html

The Toronto Review of Contemporary Writing Abroad was founded in 1981 as the Toronto South Asian Review. Later it underwent a change of name and is currently devoted to the publication of "new" Canadian (and world) writing. The term "new" is deliberately kept vague, but the bias is towards writing that traces its inspiration, at least in part, outside of the Euro-American mainstream. Published three times a year.

Submissions were also received from the following journals:

The Antigonish Review
(Antigonish, N.S.)

The Malahat Review
(Victoria, B.C.)

B & A new fiction
(Toronto, Ont.)

NeWest Review
(Saskatoon, Sask.)

The Capilano Review
(North Vancouver, B.C.)

Prairie Fire
(Winnipeg, Man.)

Event
(New Westminster, B.C.)

*The Prairie Journal of
Canadian Literature*
(Calgary, Alta.)

Exile
(Toronto, Ont.)

Queen's Quarterly
(Kingston, Ont.)

Fireweed
(Toronto, Ont.)

Storyteller
(Kanata, Ont.)

green's magazine
(Toronto, Ont.)

TickleAce
(St. John's, Nfld.)

In 2 Print
(Port Colborne, Ont.)

West Coast Line
(Burnaby, B.C.)

Kairos
(Hamilton, Ont.)

White Wall Review
(Toronto, Ont.)

Literary Performance Scenes
(Toronto, Ont.)

Windsor Review
(Windsor, Ont.)

The Journey Prize Anthology
List of Previous Contributing Authors

* Winners of the $10,000 Journey Prize

1

1989

Ven Begamudré, "Word Games"

David Bergen, "Where You're From"

Lois Braun, "The Pumpkin-Eaters"

Constance Buchanan, "Man with Flying Genitals"

Ann Copeland, "Obedience"

Marion Douglas, "Flags"

Frances Itani, "An Evening in the Café"

Diane Keating, "The Crying Out"

Thomas King, "One Good Story, That One"

Holley Rubinsky, "Rapid Transits"*

Jean Rysstad, "Winter Baby"

Kevin Van Tighem, "Whoopers"

M.G. Vassanji, "In the Quiet of a Sunday Afternoon"

Bronwen Wallace, "Chicken 'N' Ribs"

Armin Wiebe, "Mouse Lake"

Budge Wilson, "Waiting"

2

1990

André Alexis, "Despair: Five Stories of Ottawa"

Glen Allen, "The Hua Guofeng Memorial Warehouse"

Marusia Bociurkiw, "Mama, Donya"

Virgil Burnett, "Billfrith the Dreamer"

Margaret Dyment, "Sacred Trust"

Cynthia Flood, "My Father Took a Cake to France"*

Douglas Glover, "Story Carved in Stone"

Terry Griggs, "Man with the Axe"

Rick Hillis, "Limbo River"

Thomas King, "The Dog I Wish I Had, I Would Call It Helen"

K.D. Miller, "Sunrise Till Dark"
Jennifer Mitton, "Let Them Say"
Lawrence O'Toole, "Goin' to Town with Katie Ann"
Kenneth Radu, "A Change of Heart"
Jenifer Sutherland, "Table Talk"
Wayne Tefs, "Red Rock and After"

3
1991

Donald Aker, "The Invitation"
Anton Baer, "Yukon"
Allan Barr, "A Visit from Lloyd"
David Bergen, "The Fall"
Rai Berzins, "Common Sense"
Diana Hartog, "Theories of Grief"
Diane Keating, "The Salem Letters"
Yann Martel, "The Facts Behind the Helsinki Roccamatios"*
Jennifer Mitton, "Polaroid"
Sheldon Oberman, "This Business with Elijah"
Lynn Podgurny, "Till Tomorrow, Maple Leaf Mills"
James Riseborough, "She Is Not His Mother"
Patricia Stone, "Living on the Lake"

4
1992

David Bergen, "The Bottom of the Glass"
Maria A. Billion, "No Miracles Sweet Jesus"
Judith Cowan, "By the Big River"
Steven Heighton, "A Man Away from Home Has No Neighbours"
Steven Heighton, "How Beautiful upon the Mountains"
L. Rex Kay, "Travelling"
Rozena Maart, "No Rosa, No District Six"*
Guy Malet De Carteret, "Rainy Day"
Carmelita McGrath, "Silence"
Michael Mirolla, "A Theory of Discontinuous Existence"
Diane Juttner Perreault, "Bella's Story"
Eden Robinson, "Traplines"

5

1993

Caroline Adderson, "Oil and Dread"

David Bergen, "La Rue Prevette"

Marina Endicott, "With the Band"

Dayv James-French, "Cervine"

Michael Kenyon, "Durable Tumblers"

K.D. Miller, "A Litany in Time of Plague"

Robert Mullen, "Flotsam"

Gayla Reid, "Sister Doyle's Men"*

Oakland Ross, "Bang-bang"

Robert Sherrin, "Technical Battle for Trial Machine"

Carol Windley, "The Etruscans"

6

1994

Anne Carson, "Water Margins: An Essay on Swimming by
   My Brother"

Richard Cumyn, "The Sound He Made"

Genni Gunn, "Versions"

Melissa Hardy, "Long Man the River"*

Robert Mullen, "Anomie"

Vivian Payne, "Free Falls"

Jim Reil, "Dry"

Robyn Sarah, "Accept My Story"

Joan Skogan, "Landfall"

Dorothy Speak, "Relatives in Florida"

Alison Wearing, "Notes from Under Water"

7

1995

Michelle Alfano, "Opera"

Mary Borsky, "Maps of the Known World"

Gabriella Goliger, "Song of Ascent"

Elizabeth Hay, "Hand Games"

Shaena Lambert, "The Falling Woman"

Elise Levine, "Boy"

Roger Burford Mason, "The Rat-Catcher's Kiss"

168 LIST OF PREVIOUS CONTRIBUTING AUTHORS

Antanas Sileika, "Going Native"
Kathryn Woodward, "Of Marranos and Gilded Angels"*

8
1996

Rick Bowers, "Dental Bytes"
David Elias, "How I Crossed Over"
Elyse Gasco, "Can You Wave Bye Bye, Baby?"*
Danuta Gleed, "Bones"
Elizabeth Hay, "The Friend"
Linda Holeman, "Turning the Worm"
Elaine Littman, "The Winner's Circle"
Murray Logan, "Steam"
Rick Maddocks, "Lessons from the Sputnik Diner"
K.D. Miller, "Egypt Land"
Gregor Robinson, "Monster Gaps"
Alma Subasic, "Dust"